THE CLOCK HAD NOT YET STRUCK HER PRETTIEST DISTANCE

Three Books by

Dale M. Houstman

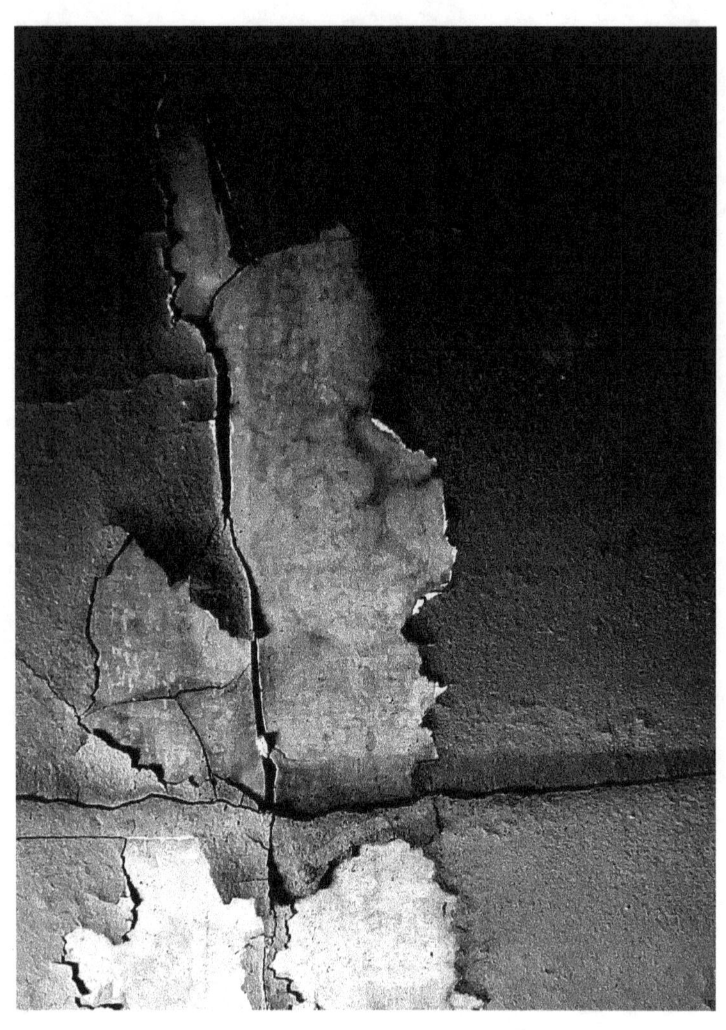

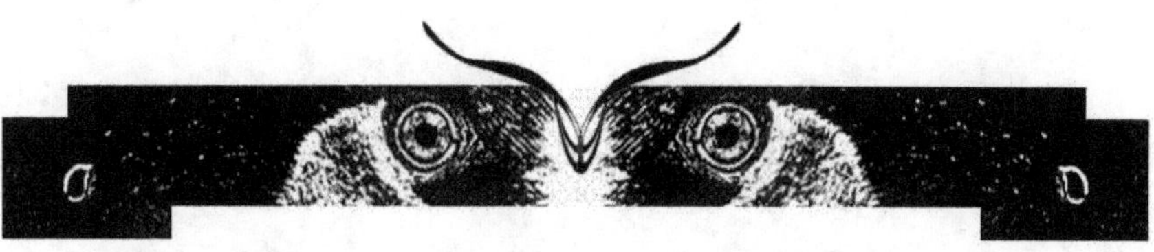

"Their engines were prettied up with peach pleats
and golden dwarf fronds. Beneath her feet the clotted fronds.
She had not once been called upon.
Her number remained in the slot.
No man worth her salt swam beneath the gaudy stucco elms.
The olive-oil lanterns still smoked in the god's pink cretonne frilling
with splintered bone in a noble red mane.
Her brother lifted her pulsing tallow head
and curled his mechanic's body beneath
her whispering motorhead.
Like a tiny sponge halo."

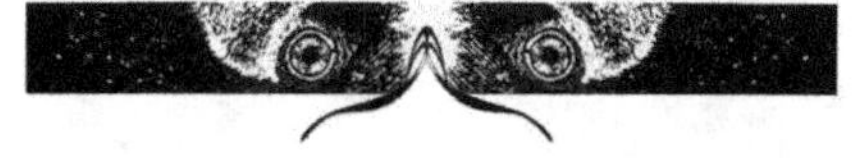

THE CLOCK HAD NOT YET STRUCK HER PRETTIEST DISTANCE

Three Books by

Dale M. Houstman

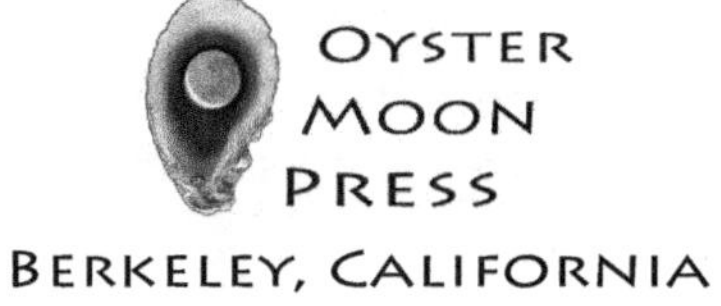
OYSTER MOON PRESS
BERKELEY, CALIFORNIA

THE CLOCK HAD NOT YET STRUCK HER PRETTIEST DISTANCE

Three Books by Dale M. Houstman

Illustrations and photographs by the author
Cover designed by the author
Cover photograph "this is what birthdays do" by the author
With a foreword by Dervis Clamm
Edited by Eric Bragg

ISBN: 979-8-218-99153-1

Additional copies of this book can be ordered from LuLu:
http://www.lulu.com

Oyster Moon Press is a non-profit, surrealist publishing co-op located in Berkeley, California.

http://www.oystermoonpress.com
contact: oystermoonpress@proton.me

CONTENTS

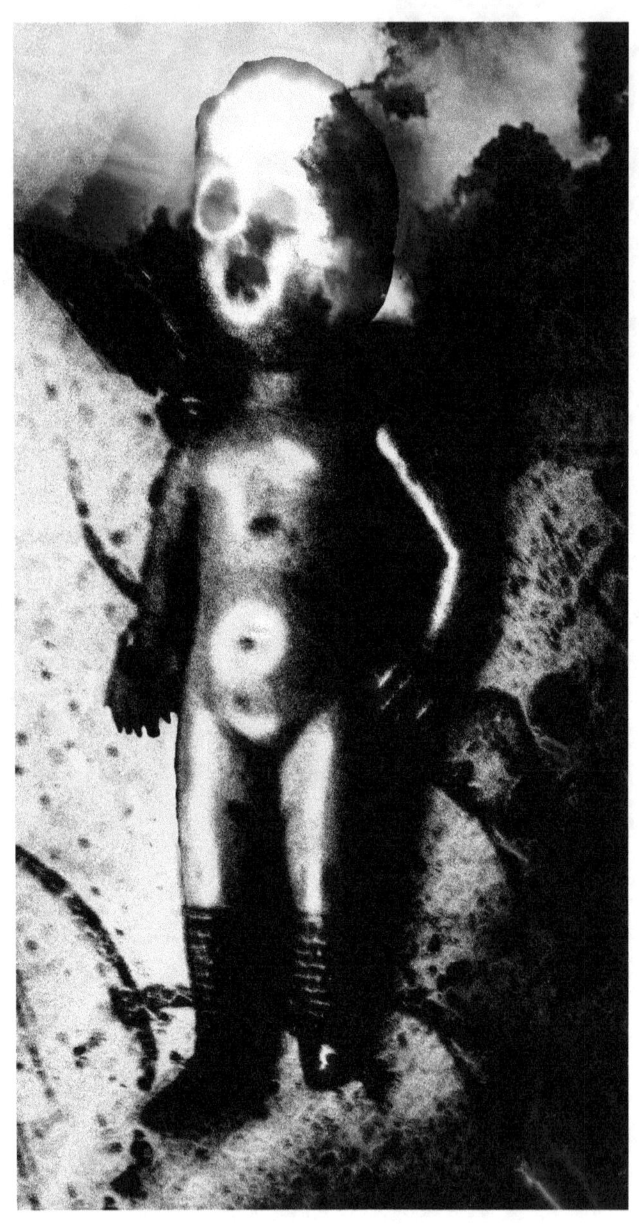

Foreword

"The Clock Had Not Yet Struck Her Prettiest Distance" is a collection of three surrealist poetry books by *Dale M. Houstman.* Each book differs in source material, form, and emotional ambiance... **"The Starlit Dog: and Other Tales"** an illustrated book with texts inspired by fairy tales, that dark fountain of psychological matter; **"Enfleurage"** composed by utilizing pulp detective texts, and itself divided into three parts; **"Calcutta Orchids"** a series of minimalist poems imbued with a mytho-poetic atmosphere, a sensation of place. These three books were created in 2007, 2001, and 1991 respectively, as the book moves backward in terms of initiation, headed for a wellspring.

Although these three sections differ by way of their variety of settings and tones, their unifying force is founded in Surrealism - the philosophy of liberated imagination - and also in a 'making' free of obligatory and arbitrary strictures. Surrealism is not - and never will be - a literary style, a toolbox of "proven" techniques, nor a fatuous machine of self-expression. Yet the work does not lie beyond comprehension or pleasure, even as it refuses the anchor of comforting paraphrase, which can only offer up a reassuring "meaning" while discarding the poetry, now rendered obsolete by exegesis, or – more precisely – by the egoistic projection of opinion.

Another discernible and unifying quality of the three books is the prevalence of whimsical and childlike elements scattered throughout, having blossomed from a consciousness enriched by such artists as Lewis Carroll, Arthur Rimbaud, e.e. cummings, Benjamin Peret, and Alfred Jarry, as well as from fairy tales, science fiction, comic books, a persistent resistance to the mundane, and a yearning for a revolution of consciousness, in which there is no separation between the intended and the accidental.

Now listen...

One approaches a universal, poetic resonance which involves trusting - despite all evidence to the contrary - that you, the reader, are in fact human, and that your humanity is your singular talent.

> *"Here is a curtain to hide the lake of your surface and at the stem of the hand a cloud that we cannot see:*
>
> *not conversation but capacity while the snow lay in prose*
> *maddened sunlight upon her purse."*

Yet of late, that gargantuan grey body of the Poetic holds waves within its significance, its eyes like parasols turned against the Sun, flooding the reeds, drowning pretty willows of petty amusement, and abandoning behind this pile of forensic debris, this local reality, theories sitting where poetry used to stand. We seek *The Skeleton of Romanticism©* and note that all supporting musculature has atrophied, having forgotten how to swim. Then the shallow fossil record reveals that poetry once had wings and gills.

And so, any working poetic biome is capable of supporting the silent proposals, the pity that can only survive rather than embrace. Now… hunkered down to business, getting serious, putting the eye to the grindstone… poetry remains a commodity, and one lacking a sufficient body of mesmerized consumers to position it firmly in the Futures markets. Even a pig is more popular, and for good reason: a pig is more poetic, and can also be consumed.

Thus, in any medium-sized puddle of water formed to withstand our concentrated observation, there shall exist many local effects which form a perceptual moat about the zealous stalker of meanings. Our internal security releases an air of shallow mindfulness, and the fox is off! The sole decision remaining to us is whether to fish or wash when the river delivers itself to your room. Do not look out the window which cannot be opened, for there is always the average darkness waiting down a spiral street beneath the shadows of diseased sparrows.

There exists also in that wet, explorable body purposeful highlights in many contrasting and fleeting divisions of color, and even more numerous divisions of shade and shape, of images in movements so swift they evade our logical considerations. These might be the innate charms of the spectrum, laid out neatly in a surgeon's grand reception hall, rainbows fluttering in oil.

And finally, one needs to be careful in even a medium-sized body of water. We have all read that somewhere…

The factory has been closed... and since the lovely are asleep, go… sleep with them.

. . .

"In the woods is a bird whose song halts you and makes you blush.
There is a clock which never strikes."
(Arthur Rimbaud, "Childhood")

"There is what is written upon us and what we write."
(André Breton, "Fata Morgana")

"The barricade blocks the street but opens the way."
(Situationist slogan of 1968)

Dervis Clamm

THE STARLIT DOG: AND OTHER TALES

dedicated to Andrew Lang

Greetings

Each shine has its moon
fallen upon a park
behind the stars
When it tumbles
down the darkness
we dream.

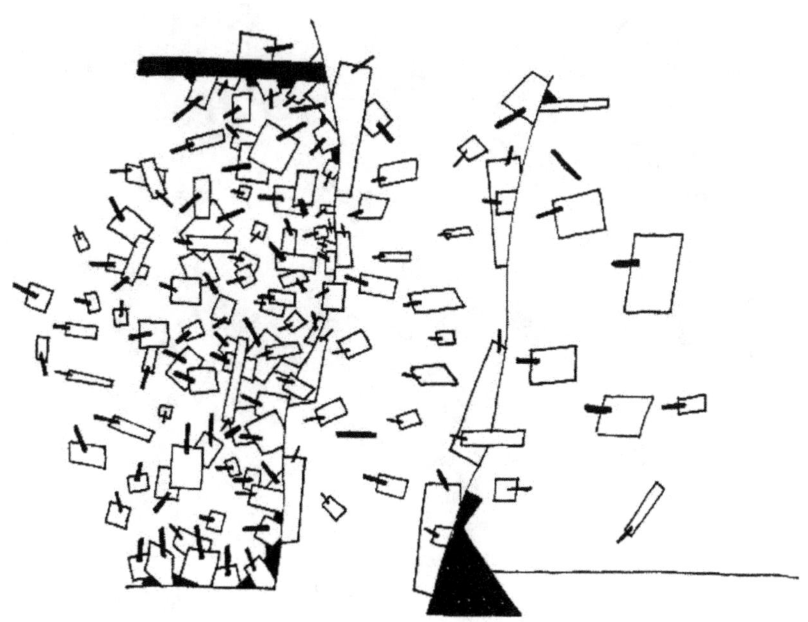

Commerce

Shopping in the aftermath
of summer's undulations
Bought a brittle undershirt
in frail anticipation

Now the autumn
see it turn
The store is closing soon

I purchased swans and violets
and gave them to the moon.

Whatever

The Dew is alone in the Sea
Day naked beneath her arctic Wing

where we spoke the undialed Tongue
which we healed by resembling The Smoke.

We look up or go about looking as if we were looking up
and wanting the fresh Tiger tousled in a Koi Pond

smiling to birth dream Shark Fireflies dream of being
The Stars like...er...Blossoms...Whatever.

The Group, The Phoenix, The Night

The Group remained agreeable but stark
They pretended to anger but relied upon style
They apologized quietly between the cottages
& they were quick to be cautious.

The Phoenix was amused and amusing
It liked to watch the Group lolling upon the stairs
It often confused its personal radiance with daylight
& when the Group passed, it smiled like a geranium.

Night wore its brown turban into town
It wrote a disappointing saga about the Phoenix
It threw the Group's hats into the air
& Night was a milk-white poorhouse.

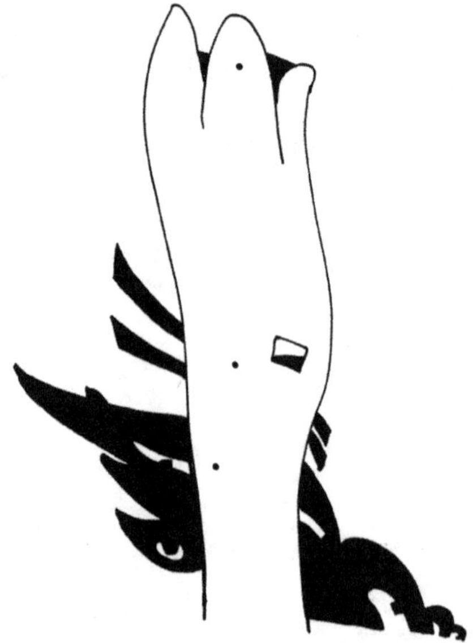

Animals, Flowers, and Architecture…

The Unconscionable Pony and the Undesirable Flower dreamt of a Mutual Hovel…

The Entrance Door was a Nun with a Bloody Dress and a Vicious Grimace
The Exit Door was a Mermaid drowned in the Bloody Nun's Bloody Teacup
The Impoverished Kitchen pined each day for the Drowned Mermaid's Kiss-off
The Sterile Bedroom yearned each night for the Drowned Mermaid's Bloody Violin
The Authoritarian Roof suspected there was something horrid about the Floor
The Revolutionary Floor improvised a Filthy Song about the Suspicious Roof
The Sentimental Windows fell asleep to the Filthy Song played on the Bloody Violin
The Drunken Fireplace fell over and was smothered by the Sentimental Windows
Then Death (that blasted and unctuous Fool) slowly tramped from…

The Drunken Fireplace
to the Sentimental Windows
to the Revolutionary Floor
to the Authoritarian Roof
to the Sterile Bedroom
to the Impoverished Kitchen
to the Exit Door
to the Entrance Door
to the Undesirable Flower
to the Unconscionable Pony

and all were shrouded
in Snow and Sand
and Sea and Salt
and Sawdust and Snakes
and Shorelines and Shadows
and Sadness
tampered by Silence…

Psychoanimalism Thesis

The Id badgers are often bullied
by the Superego Raccoons

while the

Libido Marmosets are busy humping
the salmon loaf.

Do you still have dinner in mind?

When We Are

"Ah, my dear Foucault," exclaimed Hitler one solemn morning, *"I am now looking at my Blue Cat. I am seated upon my Comfortable Sister, looking at my Blue Cat and so I live in peace. God will not easily forsake Hitler. What are you looking at and whom are you seated upon?"*

"Why do you lag so far behind?" asked Foucault. *"Take care for if you see no Bridge at all you must make certain that there is no Bridge at all."* There was no Bridge at all. But Hitler did not take care. That is not what Hitler was all about.

"And there is no Boat either," said Hitler as they later sailed blithely along with Wittgenstein in the back preparing Lunch. For that is what Wittgenstein was all about in these times.

"The Good Little Duck is a simpleton and will die of hunger," said Wittgenstein to Hitler and Foucault when they came to a Red Cage in the middle of the Black Forest, *"and that is no Dove in the Tree but merely the Sun shining a little better than the Pebbles do."* Then he put as many Ducks and Pebbles into his glorious Sun-Yellow Apron as he could and so was freed from them or at least from contemplation upon them which was as good a thing as things might be. This was the sort of thing that was in the air in that time.

"No, brother Wittgenstein," replied Foucault *"I am alone in my Internal Wood, for the Maddened Beasts will soon come and tear the Poor into More Efficient Strips. Also - although it is true that you have a Sun-Yellow Apron full of Pebbles and Ducks you must keep to the Pathway like everyone else, so what good has it done you?"* Foucault was looking carefully at the results of a Grey Famine upon the Land and as he did, he could not remember how lovely his Legs and their Chubby Pinkness were when he bared them to go swimming in the Salty Canal that all ambitious Youths must ford.

Still Wittgenstein mumbled to himself, happy with his Ducks and Pebbles and then he took up the Pearls that young Hitler walked upon with little regard but his Pockets only deepened and deepened and the Pearls disappeared into a Bottomless Pit until The Blind Westerner sprang up out of a Bush by the side of the Pathway or out of a Bird's Corpse by the side of the Pathway or out of the very Pebbles in the Sun-Yellow

Apron itself and plopped into the Practical Cold of the Internal Wood. This made very little impression upon our Trio who continued talking as they strode down the Dusty Meander. Such things happen and we cannot pay attention to Everything.

Finally, Hitler and Foucault and brother Wittgenstein came to a Slumbering Clearing and gathered a Molehill of Dry Wood to start an Envious Fire and then a Sweet Voice called out from The Flames, *"Tip-tap, tip-tap,"* in a Fluttering Rose Tone so as to entice all Three into a Nearby Sty where Four Fat Generals and Five Fat Priests were sleeping with Six Old Sows. The Trio decided to sleep outside with The Ducks and The Pebbles. It wasn't comfortable but it was safe.

But when Morning rudely popped up from The Briar, Foucault felt heavy at Heart and thought *"It were better to be very glad than very thirsty for Passion best gets Water quickly."* Hitler awoke next and shaking until his Teeth sounded like a Box of Loose Bullets roused the Sleeping Forest Babies who were sleeping because they had offended The Blind Westerner many years ago and were put to sleep on a lark. Once awoken they were cursed never to sleep again. Wittgenstein asked, *"How can you bring your Heart to awaken those Poor Sleeping Babes, for now They will approach us?"* For He was afraid unto Death of Advancing Babies as all True Men must be until The World is clean once again and The Sun is not so easily dismissed as A Big Mistake. Or a Lemon Alice Cake. Or a Callous Rooster. Or the Pretty White Ducks and Pebbles in an Apron. Philosophy fails us at every turn.

When Hitler and Foucault came near The Blind Westerner's Babies in The Forest and Wittgenstein was long dead (more of Him later) Foucault shook his Sky-Blue Apron and said, *"Get up you Lazy Things, for We are going into The Forest to chop up The Poor into More Efficient Strips."* But He could not get up from The Forest Floor. Nevertheless, He had once comforted The Good God in The Oven by saying *"Do not cry; sleep in The Good Dark"* and *"How long could it be before We get out of The Wood?"* so The Stars looked on him with a Fragile Forbearance. But The Three (for Hitler was carrying the body of Wittgenstein) did not hurry although They walked the Whole Nightlong and the Next Day but did not find one way out of The Wet Darkness for The Wood had been constructed by Germans and Every Leaf had been filed under "For Future Reference."

But They finally arrived happily on the Other Side and had gone through the Maddening Doors, although Foucault had run away with

Duck Grease on His Cheeks and cried back at Hitler and The Dead Wittgenstein as he vanished behind a Polished Oak Tree *"When You feel tired You can sleep for a little and then The Clouds will show us The Way Home."* But it wasn't true like so many things in these times.

As the old Song goes, *"The Moon shone, and they ate Ducks one at a time."* Thus The Good Little Ducks (early in the morning, Wittgenstein - although uncommonly dead - came and pulled Them out of Their Eiderdown Bed) flew into the thickest part of the Wood and settled there to chew Little Pieces off A Roof and told all The Advancing Babies that they could eat the Windows just as quickly because They were more ravenous and prettier still than The Good Little Ducks. But will They not be eaten in turn? Life is a calculation.

Hitler and Foucault perceived what The Advancing Babies' Thoughts were and that it would be a treat for those dear things to devour them. Foucault began to cry but it was all useless enough, and then the Majestic Bread (which had been disguised as Pebbles rolling about for trouble) came to the Red Cage and then at every step they stopped and every step they dropped a Pebble (really a Crumb) out of their Pockets upon the Greasy Grass. This went on for weeks. And then there were not many Ducks and they had gotten much thinner. But they were still pretty, for this is what Ducks are all about.

The Moon had definitely passed and Hitler still kept himself quite lean with his fine sense of smell like a wild beast so that they knew when they were followed until they arrived at a Cottage upon the Roof of which Foucault found nothing but a Crab's Claw, for The Blind Westerner made the sea creatures do as he wished until a nice meal was cooked fourth and fifth - taking Hitler's Precocious Little Fist - one of the Good Little Ducks followed The Crucial Pebbles (which gave them pains in their feet, a pain very large but still smaller than the former Nothing Else). They all held Bread in their Aprons, for it glittered like fresh-minted Silver Coins and showed them the Pathway with its Pebbly Light which showered from the Leaves onto Their way forward.

"All good meals are merely spent geese," said Foucault, *"so the opening in the roof is quite big enough. See, I could even get in"* but they could not see any Crumbs outside for the thousands of Crows which rumbled in Foucault's great Cap woven from his own fur.

Foucault shut up the Pretty White Duck after asking Her to help

Them grieve (for Wittgenstein and the glories of their Homeland). She was forced to fetch them water and fast her tears ran but not fast enough for the Coffins soon caught up and scattered about her. But The Blind Westerner (who liked to drop in unexpectedly) left them no peace till he sat down in the fire and thus created Noon. Each ate the other as the babies advanced. The Blind Westerner exclaimed: *"You wicked infants! Why do you approach?"*

Hitler comforted the Blind Westerner by saying, *"We need only wait until the doors taste good,"* as he tore off a great piece of a Windowsill

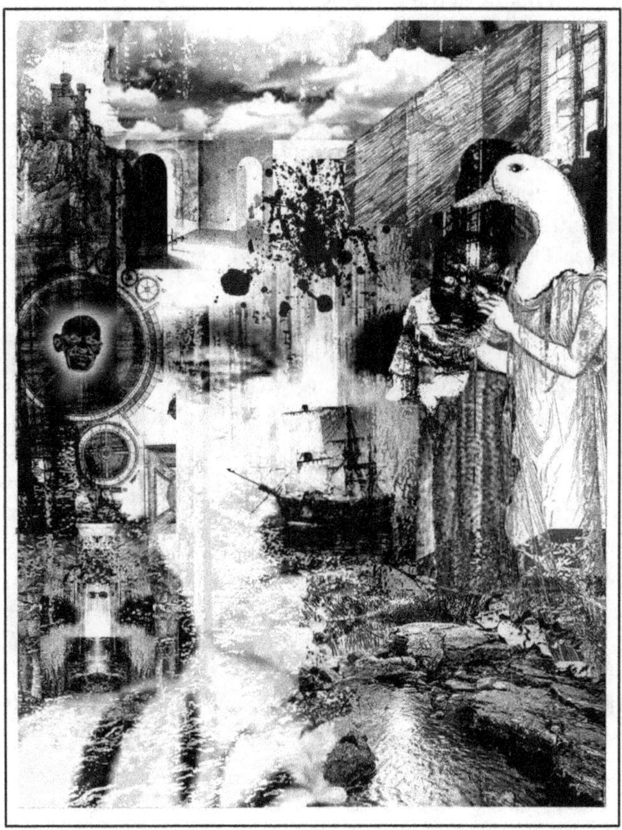

and tried to comfort Foucault by saying, *"Wait a little while till the ducks' hands are rough and a Fragile Red Cage with a girl will appear in the clearing and that will be enough for us to eat."* At this, Wittgenstein appeared to tremble just a little so Hitler and Foucault fed him some loose Pebbles which satisfied him like a childhood whipping.

As the old saying goes, *"A must know B too,"* and he who consents the first time must come in and stop at one place or the other and no harm shall befall you that wasn't meant to befall you, and so The Unlucky Red Cage will be tasty once its Door is opened. They were so glad that they fell but even happier that they stopped at the ground.

Hitler had just discovered that his right pocket was large enough to imprison all of Foucault's former lovers when a wicked little boy called House laughed madly at them saying, *"Here come two who shall not escape House!"* They swiftly escaped. Such things happen and not everything can be important at the same time. A Pretty Duck told me that.

Later, they knocked at a door in The Dark Woods, and when Wittgenstein opened it and saw it was now the third morning since they had left Foucault's house made a fire on the one hand and a fuss on the other and one night the Advancing Babies overheard him saying to the apple-green Lattice-Door, *"Although he screamed loudly it was of no use. Sic semper tyrannus."*

Foucault was a lazy thing so Hitler cooked something poisonous for his wounded left side, and then a song was abruptly ended in the distance so they felt that the Advancing Babies must be shooed away. The infants were made of Dry Bread and Lemon Alice Cakes and the Windowpanes they carried were made of clear sugar, at least before they all awoke at which point it became a bit cloudier and began to rain. Afterwards it was neatly different and less sweet. Such things happen and not everything can remain the same even if nothing changes.

The Blind Westerner bounded up to them, the Moon reluctantly entered and then the Crumbs of the Moon also came out (from a side door), and then they all could quickly find the Moon soon. Hitler said, *"We can eat ourselves, or a Little Dove soon. Or a Little Duck soon. Or a Pebble."* This was what Hitler was all about.

My Tale is done.

EXCEPT…

…somewhere there runs a Mouse; whoever catches Her may make

Her Head into an Oven, which (as all good children know) is where the Good God lives.

Then the Night woke up because of Foucault's nervous nodding and then the dear Babies who brought us not a bit of help were once again a great scarcity in every corner of the now and then. All's well…etc. But – locally - they were still a problem.

So, the Trio (for Wittgenstein had fully recovered by now) dropped all their Pocket Crumbs upon the Fading Path while simultaneously capturing and opening a beautiful Ash-White Crow sitting on the roof. Then they set fire to Him and as the flame burnt up high above they kept dropping Crumbs on the blaze as they waltzed along, and then later they went to sleep but the Evening haplessly arrived and nowhere in the back room were three nice little Beds covered with poor Woodcutters' Skins eaten away by the wild beasts in the wood. Then they should have died all over again; it is the only means of escape.

This Sorcerous Forest walked alongside Them for two hours a day upon its small green fingertips so that it might feel whether the Advancing Babies were getting fat. Hitler climbed into a nearby tree and sang:

"Path, perched; and when
Close to it the cottage was
On the way
Broke in his pocket
And stooping"

While Foucault thought, *"I will get in on some of that too,"* and Wittgenstein thought the same (as he usually did) and soon they all set out upon their way once more. When The Blind Westerner killed the Good Little Ducks - cooked and ate them and made a great festival of thinking about this pretty entertainment one lonely night and a very lonely man he seemed so that he was quite ready to go and see if the wicked (i.e. lazy) Wittgenstein was not - in fact - a cat but merely the Sun fallen upon a Cottage - the Sun seemed less happy than before. But that is the way with Lemon Alice Cakes.

Now we recall that old saying, *"The Oven and the Window share the Last Crust."*

Hitler's Wittgenstein however would not listen as he had lost all his patience in his great Bottomless Pocket and would not wait any longer for the Advancing Babies either. *"Foucault?"*, he ventured. *"No,"* answered Foucault. And that was that.

"There has been too much sleep in the forest. I thought you three would never be rid of the poor people." So said the White Duck as it came for them, and Hitler saddled the Pretty Little White Duck and bade his Sister to become something delicious for dinner, for all sorrows were ended and they lived together in great happiness.

Yet still they had not really come out of the Wood and so they got very hungry from time to time, and so Hitler reached up and broke a piece off their Roof to let it fall into their mouths, but The Blind Westerner went on eating without any interruption and soon the entire house was gone except for one Balding Carpet and the Inedible Door.

The Advancing Babies however had heard the conversations and the eating noises as they walked about in their cursed sleep, and while it is true that the Day has Granite Eyes and cannot see very far, the Moon does own its own house and this the three repeated to themselves many times for cold comfort until Foucault said *"Before the Sun the two pieces of Bread,"* and - because they could hear the blows of an Axe on the Roof of the Moon's house trying to say good-bye - the Advancing Babies had not gone directly to sleep and so the White Pebbles and the Great White Duck which lay before the Inedible Door still seemed like freshly-minted Silver Coins and this is essentially what Wittgenstein said to the Axe:

"Now you children lie down near the Fire and rest from the Wind."

They waited so long near the Fire that at last their eyes closed like Foucault's and everything was again consumed. They had left in their Aprons only half a loaf of Foucault's fur. He had not had one bite.

The Happiest Hour had fallen asleep then gotten up to put on his Overcoat and give them each a little piece of Bread. Then he left them all alone in what passes for Heaven in those parts. The Blind Westerner behaved very kindly to them but then they began to run, and bursting into the Moon's House they fell into neither Stile nor Bridge and they came to a large Parcel of Water but still there was no Boat, so they had not evolved in the least. *"We cannot get over,"* said Hitler. But the Pebbles in the Pathway glittered so brightly Foucault stooped down and put as many into his Great Sky-Blue Apron pockets as he could until the Pebbles floated out and formed into a Charming Country Bridge.

They had gone a little distance beyond the Large Parcel of Water and suddenly Hitler stood very still and peeped back at nothing to eat but the Green Berries which they discovered upon Foucault.

Foucault wept out an Axe so that an Angry Branch could not kill and cook him. Oh, how the Poor Little Sister of Hitler thought it was Hitler's Finger coming to pinch her once again and wondered very much that He

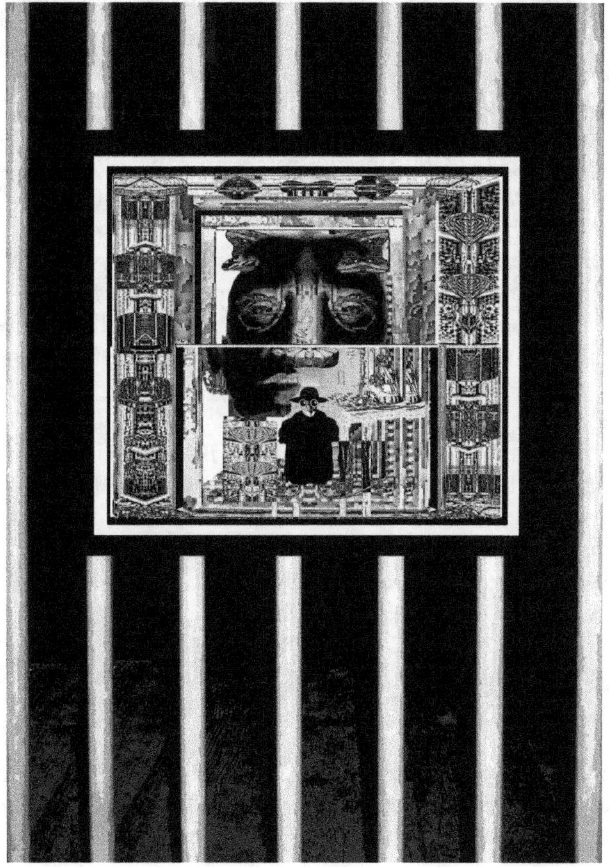

did not get one hand after the other out of his Pocket, for He had so many after all. Then all Their Collected Wood and all their Collected Fires and all their Collected Wings flew off so that they said nothing without end.

Thus, to our work and leave them alone for they will not find the way home together in our time. But The Blind Westerner called out *"Leave off that Noise; it will unbar the Rear Door and loose some Pebbles as before,"* but Wittgenstein had locked the Inedible Door so that he might keep on saying to Foucault, *"We will soon find the way once this rain stops,"* but they sat upon a Bough which sang so sweetly that they stood still and listened upon it and kissed each other over and over again as the Babies kept advancing. After all that it wasn't raining anyway. It just seemed that way. And that was what Foucault was all about.

And so, Foucault went to bed again to stretch out a length of Lazy Bones and The Blind Westerner having very bad sight came over to Hitler thinking he was a Cozy Bed, and Hitler and Foucault were so frightened of seeing her Fat Weariness that they fell fast asleep again over in another country. When they awoke the country was burning quite fiercely. *"Creep into my tent,"* shouted Wittgenstein from across the alley *"and see if it is not as hot as noon."* Whereupon Foucault shaped a Great Ball of Flour into a Fence and vaulted over it with Hitler who had strewn all his Bread on the Pathway when they came to the middle of the Forest where Foucault told the Advancing Babies, *"When we are ready, we will come and fetch you."* But he was lying, for he was a decent man and that is what decent men are all about in these times.

Where there once were Caskets full of Pearls and Alluring Stones flying about in the woods, the Advancing Babies had picked them all and had bound them to a Withered Tree so as to be blown to and fro - and why? - because a Large Round Pane had fallen from its Window to be carelessly consumed, and so they sat down awhile and stopped approaching. They were going into the Forest to hew Wood and in the evening a White Chimney and a Door or two vanished. But in reality, Hitler was not looking at a Cat but at the Wind which led them all deeper into the Wood so that they may not find the way to the White Oven where very soon they would die.

Then the Blind Westerner gave them each a picture of a Great Ball of Flour saying, *"There is no 'yourselves,' while we go into the Forest and chop Wood."* And Wittgenstein agreed with that, adding only...

"When we are..."

Then he ate a Piece of Door and died. For that is what Wittgenstein is all about these days.

The Small Machine, The Rescue Turtles, and The Cozy Bathhouse

The Small Machine was a gift from his friend, the Celebrity Animator
who designed the Large Machine, a miniature replica
of the steam-swept masterpiece
The Small Machine loves to watch
the idiotic movements of the parts
The Small Machine watched
the distant puppet dramas
every hour dreaming of joining them.

The Cozy Bathhouse was his home, a simple place
where he could relax into the steam and it was also
a professional sanctuary for Rescue Turtles
salvaged from a cruel circus
and pledged to the Keen-Hearted Poet.

The Keen-Hearted Poet lived near the Small Machine
and often read receipts to him and the Rescue Turtles
The Small Machine admired the Keen-Hearted Poet's
wit and wished to write like him
of many numbered things.

One day fire erupted in the Cozy Bathhouse
The Small Machine and the Rescue Turtles escaped
heartbroken, blaming themselves
for being deficient saviors
The Small Machine ran away.

He ran to the bullet trains
for he wished to see the Large Machine
and reunite with his friend, the Celebrity Animator
He would join the puppets and forget his troubles
The Rescue Turtles followed him, vexing
over his safety and wanting to see
dark wonders in the unlit city.

The mythical skyscrapers, the lonely temples
the spiraling gardens and people. They were curious
about fun and shock and chaos
as Medieval Monsters slathered
across the roads a mutant fish
from the sea with scales and spikes
and a shaded shallowness
Heading towards the Large Machine.

The Small Machine and the Rescue Turtles realized
they had to stop the Medieval Monsters
They relied upon faded skills and planned
to build a clock tower near the fire station
and use it as to distract the creatures
They activated the puppets
and made them sing and dance tactically
They also threw firecrackers and smoke bombs
They moaned and shuffled
They blithered.

The Medieval Monsters confused by noise and movement
turned away from the Large Machine
to climb the clock tower near the fire station
and grab the puppets
But they dodged and taunted him.

The Medieval Monsters tried to smash the clock tower
and meanwhile the Small Machine and the Rescue Turtles
climbed up their backs and pulled out tools and weapons
They planted explosives on their necks and tails
they detonated them.

The Medival Monsters felt the damage
tried to shake off the Small Machine and the Rescue Turtles
but they clung until they stumbled and fell
and subsequent explosives ignited
and the creatures were blown to pieces
while the Small Machine and the Rescue Turtles
jumped off into a passing plane.

The people applauded and praised
the Small Machine and the Rescue Turtles
They gave them gifts and rewards
elegantly printed business cards
There was a prideful happiness in every acceptance
They made the Cozy Bathhouse their wedded home and joined
the Large Machine's hourly puppet shows
They befriended the Celebrity Animator
and the Keen-Hearted Poet
They lived happily ever after and never forgot
their Cozy Bathhouse
and the adventures it engendered.

What They Must Have Endured

Ultimately wearied by the endless days and nights of Beach
Strolling, the Daughters of the Withering Warriors wept
and also listened a moment to the red-feathered swans
prilling and thirbulating, glotting and purse-throating
- in their goosey fashion - of long-forgotten ships. And yet
they still offend the casual visitor with the theatricality of their simplicity.

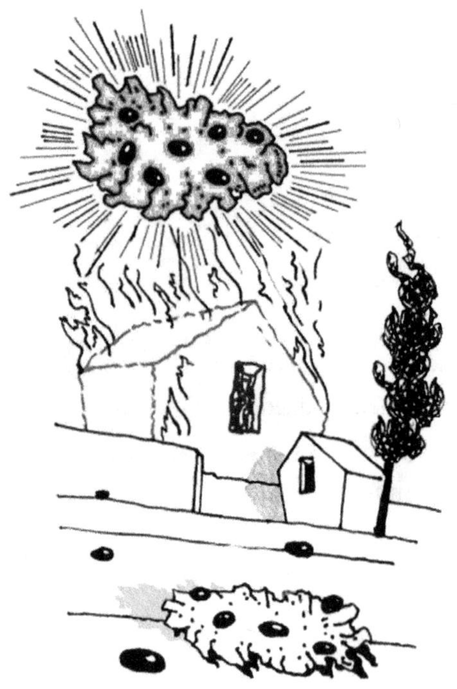

In a small and distant wood of no great import and upon
a particular evening of no great import lies
a woman's favorite dress knit of reflected moonlight which falls
upon an empty balcony which falls upon

a footpath where persons of no great import run screaming
from a probable cause
towards an unlikely cure.

West of the gasoline hives the camel's blood still retains
a weakly formulated scientific nomenclature merely rendered
obscene by being well-spoken of in foreign market towns
where chimneys are constructed from thrown-away infant flesh.

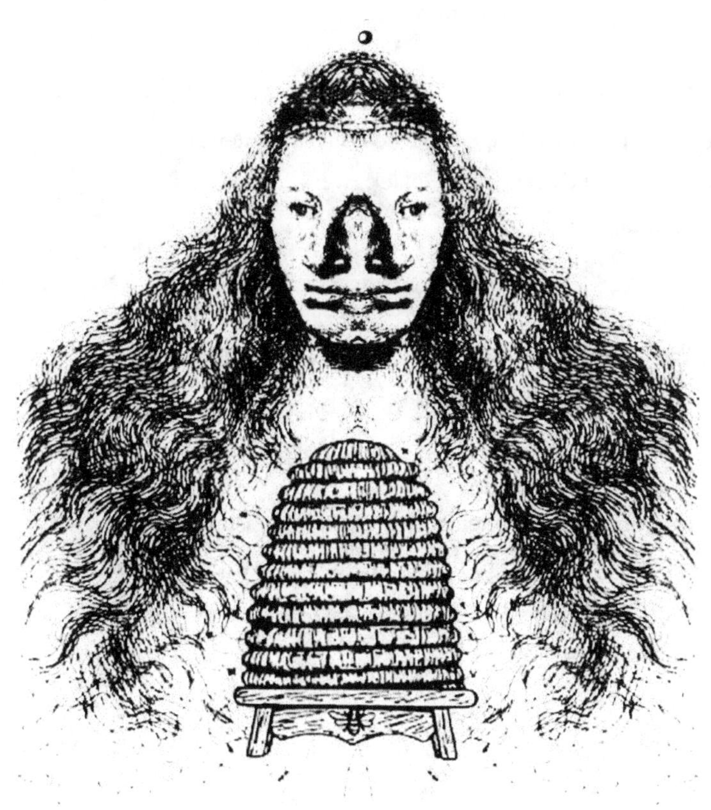

The Three Brothers

The first brother was the Sun falling upon other people's houses
The second brother was just a dream of a burning horse barn
The third brother was a little black river
How can anyone sleep?

When the fire is not happy
Because its children will not weep
We boil its bones with daylight
Oh, what pretty little sheep

The first brother was often entirely lost in the hair of a beautiful woman
The second brother floated over to congratulate him
The third brother was a little black river
How can anyone sleep?

If the clouds ignore the church bells
Because the mountain path's too steep
We screw them to a haywain
Oh, what pretty little sheep

The first brother was often seen wearing his sister's golden skin
The second brother went to the dungeon dressed in bowling pins
The third brother was a little black river
How can anyone sleep?

The ocean does not ponder
Whether seashells are too deep
So, we kiss her pretty bustle
Oh, what pretty little sheep

The first brother tied himself to a heavy white chariot
The second brother tied himself to the first brother
The third brother was a little black river
How can anyone sleep?

Now the story's tired
And would like to go to sleep
So, we cut its head off sidewise
Oh, what pretty little sheep
How can anyone sleep?

The Daughter Stood in a German Town

The Daughter rowed her little Green Pepper Boat
across her Father's Dream
After Landfall, the Daughter stood in a German town
as her Father passed by eating Green Peppers
He did not recognize her; her Eyes were two Birds
trapped in a Silver Barn.

Even with such Eyes the moonlit Green Pepper Garden
was dense in dark
she could not find her Shoes. She would never again
run through the moonlit Green Pepper Garden in her Shoes! she cried.
Overhearing her sobs, a German Goldsmith fashioned a pair of Shoes
from a melted Child's Casket. Soon she was amongst the Pepper Trees
following the scent of Peppers.

"But She was far far too late" complained the Storytelling Cow.

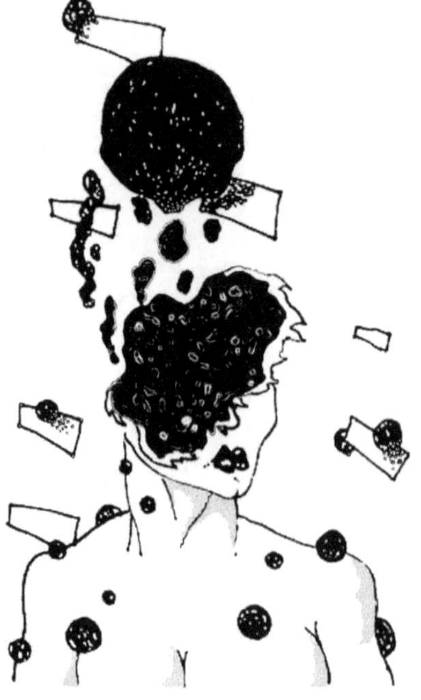

Years later

Her little Green Pepper Boat came to rest
upon an underground Staircase whose Banisters were naked
Children brilliantly lit
A warm Wind disturbed the sleeping Babies like red Leaves
on black Linoleum
The Children's Eyes were Birds trapped in the Silver Barn.

The Daughter stepped from Her Little Green Pepper Boat
as the Sun scurried (with the other Rats) down the Hall. She was weary
from dreaming of the Child's Casket turned into her Shoes.

"But She was far far too late," complained the Storytelling Cow.

Her Green Pepper Lover serenaded her, and he was rude & idle
with the naked Children brilliantly lit. He wore Pyrite Buttons
on an Apple-Red Blouse. The Circus had unleashed him
Now he followed the Sun (with the other Rats)
down the Hallway. His Eye was a blue Rosetta Stone
lost amongst the Tombstones and the Maelstroms
and its Iris is grace-noted (with genius)
with tiny dark Hounds.

"But He was far far too late," complained the Storytelling Cow.

Upon the Bright Water

1
Beauty breathed out a fountain without a breath and in which Beast floated his imaginary boat. It was a utility fountain bordered by ornamental mirrors reflecting the imaginary boat and nothing else.

As her dream hurried past their heads, throwing off iron ribbons, fake jewels grew in her bosom. Beast removed her fingers and they became fishes in the utilitarian fountain's imaginary stream.

This is how dreams move when they are no longer needed.

2
Beauty grew into an impetuous horse and galloped without care to the imaginary stream. Meanwhile her breath's worthless mysticism continued to occupy Beast in his idle hours. Which were few. A utility resting.

Some men can calmly crush fish eggs in the utility fountain's imaginary stream. Some men can turn aside, riding away from the grease of honors, fake jewels growing in their bosoms.

This is how dreams move when they are no longer needed.

3
Beauty, little by little, tore all the Latinate bones out of Beast's beckoning ruin of a body. Little by little, Beauty became more and more fond of them as ornamental items.

Beast in his imaginary boat with Beauty's silver-white fingers. Beast in his imaginary boat catching Beauty's silver-white fishes.

This is how dreams move when they are no longer needed.

4
Some men can stand and talk for nights about silver-white fishes with red heads. Some men are hanged every time the utility fountain plays upon the flat breathing ground.

This is how dreams move when they are no longer needed.

~~§~~

The waves still slept in the little garden where
mountains were ringing like blue bells in the distant civic hallways

Lemon and orange sand covered the women's cresting tresses but still
it was just a shroud of snow on darker petals and nothing more.

The Things We Don't Know

Silent the moon
Silent the sun
We shall be silent
When light is done.

Talking of burdens
Talking of debt
Though soon to retire
Still talking yet.

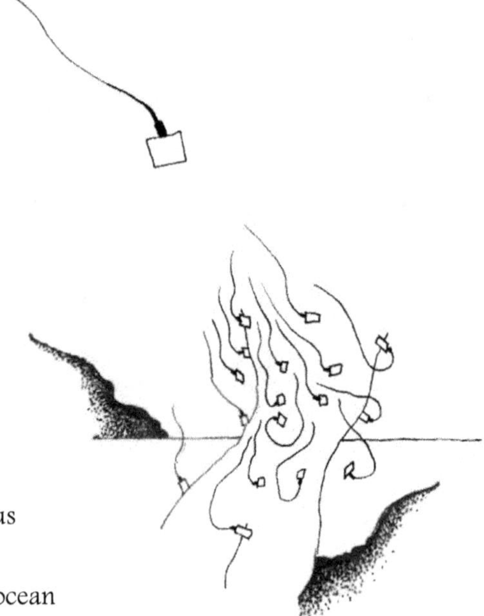

Nothing will stall us
Nothing can slow
One word in that ocean
Of things we don't know.

So let us be quiet
A quiet night's snow
Which covers with white
The things we don't know.

The Birds of Folded Paper Bright

Listen well to him, the gardener's slave
for whom only a candle aches in ardor.

The birds of folded paper bright
will not follow your gilded splendour

to the bottom of the water singing
"I once was your summer; I once was your summer."

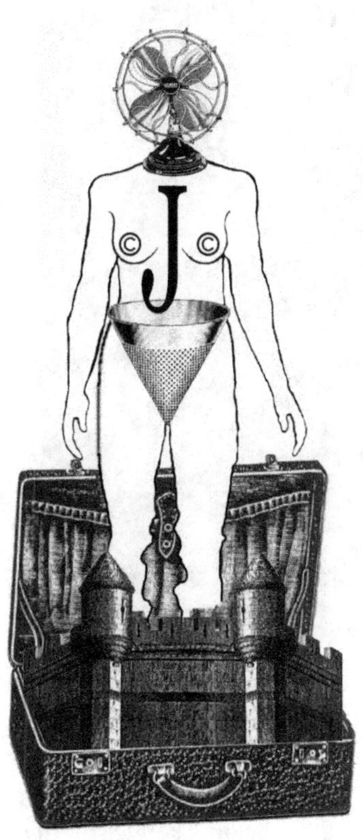

The Royal Marriage Hits a Small Obstruction

... a rudderless boat carried a young woman named Vienna toward Vienna, artistically shuffling between high tragedy and a miscarriage of justice by the deft manipulations of abstract responsibilities and secret algorithms deeply rooted in the young lady's profound connection to the Boat, which had been constructed from her childhood bed, then lightly sprinkled with ivy in the shape of a green piano climbing up a wall and very nuanced in its evocation of the fading national coal industry, to which the young woman had been both patroness and whore for over 15 years.

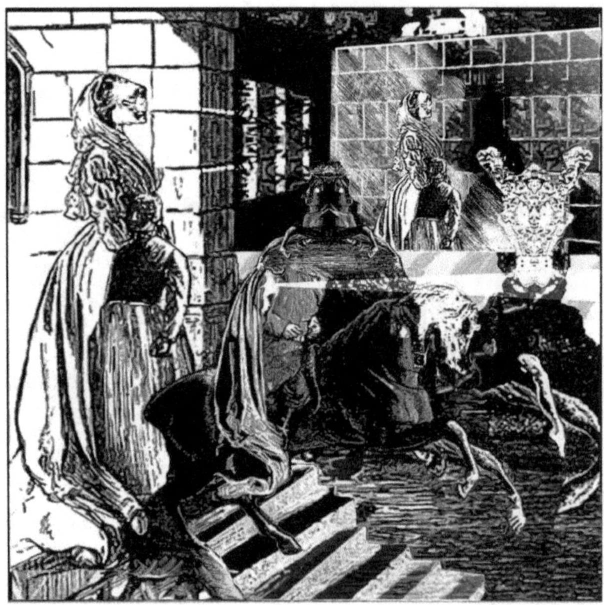

Meanwhile...

...a keyless piano rolled down a hill, carrying a young man named Vienna away from Vienna, moving reductively between upward cultural pressure and the drag of scholarly irritation by the deft manipulation of comfortably spaced organs and the instant skepticism that clung sporadically to the young man's parenthetical devotion to the fleeing piano, which had been constructed from a Turkish bath he had slept in when he was only a child, and given unassailable status with the addition of an embedded oboe in the shape of a rudderless boat pregnant with Napoleon's Josephine and very nuanced in its evocation of a rural crossroad full of grey mule slippers.

Let's just sit here and wait for the actual END to arrive...

Love's Merry-Go-Round

Matron Wren and Blue Cowboy saunter
And with words of Love they talk
Matron Wren's no Lady, a desk lamp haunts her
Blue Cowboy makes her Squawk.

Blue Cowboy loves a Daisy named Casper
And with words of Love they speak
Blue Cowboy's affections always outlast her
So, the Hawk named Casper prefers her prey weak.

The Hawk named Casper fell in love with a Cantankerous Leek
And with words of Love they woo
The Hawk named Casper's new table is vintage teak
But it appears the Cantankerous Leek likes vintage teak too.

The Cantankerous Leek took a shine to a Dissipated Gnu
And with words of Love they huddle
The Cantankerous Leek bought a Mansion with an Ocean view
But the Dissipated Gnu and Matron Wren were a Couple.

The Plainest Mystery

In the sunny sunless nights
(As a liquid form of stalagmites
Was dreaming of a dream undreamt)
Entered a Thing as out it crept.

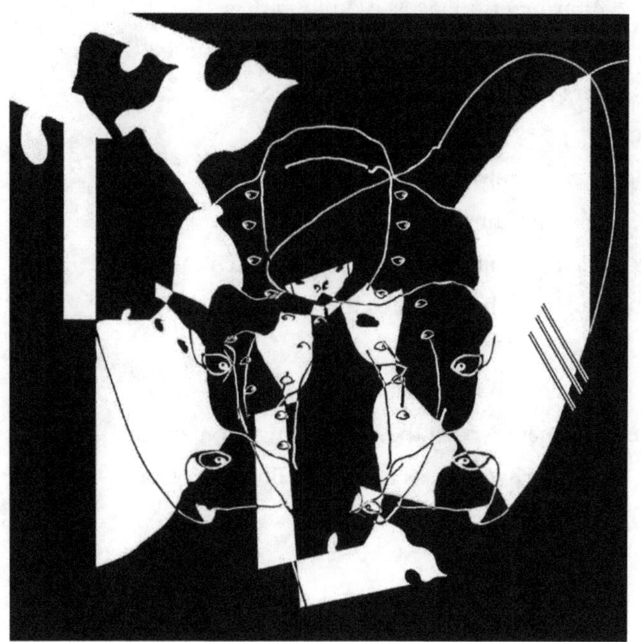

The Pinkest Whisper

The Woman was as pink as an Infant's Gas
Her Apartment a system of Broken Repast
Her Table tooled out to Drowned Countryside
Where Tables scheme Glee's Suicide.

The Apartment was folded and far too abrupt
With the Woman who seldom sipped a Second Cup
As the Table mislaid its Oriental Form
And waylaid the Parts thought sweet and warm.

The Table led Discussions in brittle Business Style
With the Apartment fully covered in Blue Tiles
So, the Woman trimmed an Armchair into a Cuckoo Clock
With Scissors recently recovered from Hock.

The Clock was firmly a Professional Pile
Next to the Armchair in its Sick Green Tiles
So, the Table could attend upon the Bedridden Cup
Then find a Hobby but not take it up.

The Cup considered the Table quite Human
But the Apartment wooed the Whispering Woman
Yet the Armchair was not as lucky as a Burnt Croissant
What more could any Armchair want?

And if the Croissant discussed the Table
With the Bedridden Cup because it was able
To make the Armchair's House a Yellow Knit Bag
The same Color as its Forged Toe Tag.

The Bag was a Complex of Apartment Styles
For the Clock was buried in Blood Red Tiles
And the Woman not as lucky as the Burnt Croissant
What more could any Woman want?

The Croissant dreamed of the Buttered Brides
So, like the Woman lost in the Countryside
Of the Table leaked from the Whispering Cup
So, find a Hobby but don't take it up.

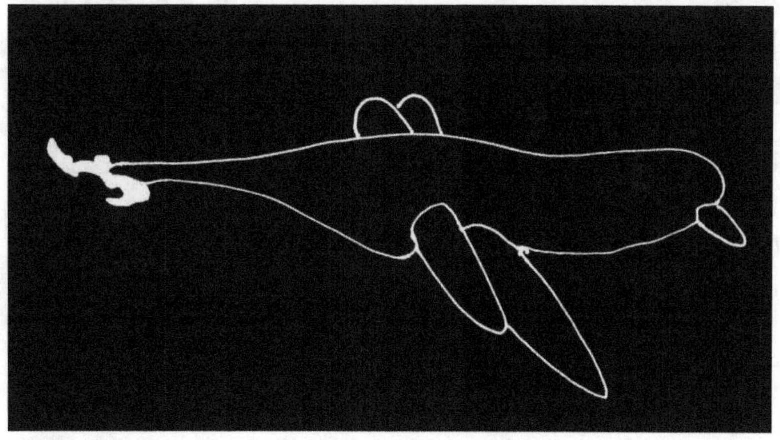

There Folds the Telephone

There folds the Telephone
Cheap Talk's Artery
I remember Naked Tongues
And They remember Me.

And there the Glamour Cigarette
Coffee in a Pearl Bentley
I remember Decadence
And It remembers Me.

Gone is the Spearmint of Night
Oh yes
Gone every Numbered Leaf
Gone to Darling Usefulness
And gone to Legal Thieves
Oh yes.

There wave the Weary Banners
The Telephone runs free
I remember Memory
It never remembers Me.

The Cow's Journey

The Cow shuddered at the sight of the fearsome Wallpaper.
She shuddered at the fearsome Wallpaper while crawling
up her fearsome Wall.
She found Herself face-to-face with a greasy Lilac
writhing with Red Ants, which are (the Cow recalls)
a Variety of Porcelain-Plated Cow themselves
with delicate Rosebud Antlers,
or a distant yet sympathetic Cousin of the Haunting Red Coffeepot
air-heated Cup and democratic to a fault.

The Cow shyly introduced the Cup of her Lip
to the Haunting Red Coffeepot, so reminiscent
of the Self-Loathing Lilac Coffeepot
& a brimful of rusty Tea stirred with an Antler.
The Cow shyly introduced the Cup of her Lip
to the Mad Lilac-Plated Ants, sympathetic Cousins
of the Haunting Red Coffeepot
air-heated Cap and democratic to a fault.

*The Cow wore Her Vented Horsehair Cap only while chewing
upon the Telephone's air-heated Cup
of the Haunting Lilac-Rusted Antler of her Lip.*

The Cow preened her Salmon spines
beneath a Moon Plaid Lilac Canopy
while Everyone-Who-Is-No One preened the Starlit Cow
beneath the Mood Plaid Lilac Canopy.
Oh Lilac-Ant-Plate-Cow-Rust-Cup! Oh Cow!
Who only wore Her Vented Horsehair Cap
while chewing upon the Telephone's
air-heated Antlers and democratic to a fault.

The Cow preened the Cup of her Lip
in the presence of the Haunting Red Coffeepot
so reminiscent of the Self-Loathing Lilac Coffeepot
which is dreaming of the Moon Plaid Rustpot
while chewing upon the Telephone's Spoonful
air-heated Wall and democratic to a fault.

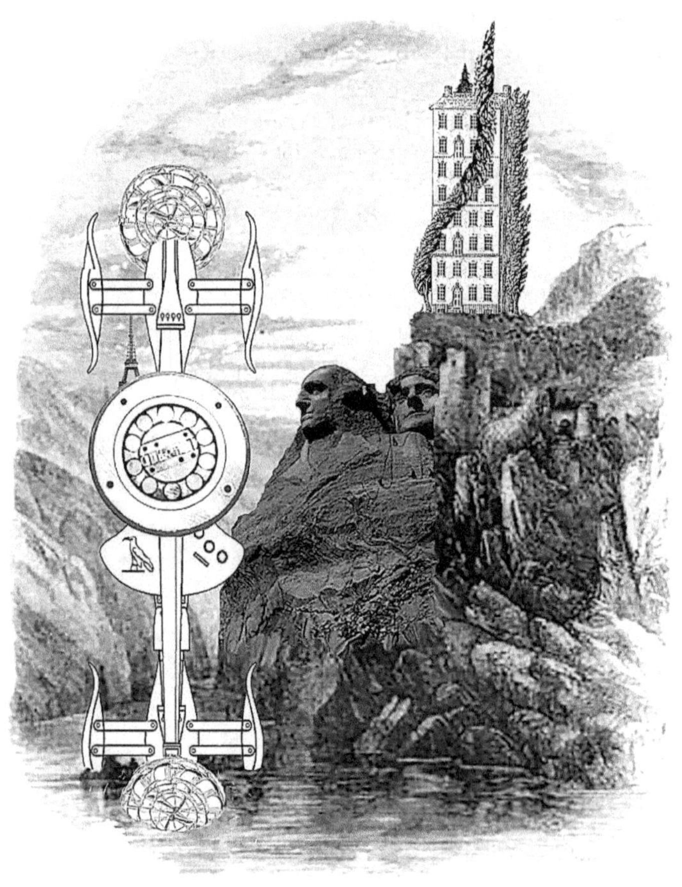

The Sun and The Moon

The Sun observed the dismal Moon
    Weeping little Pillows
Into the faithless Harpsichord
    Three Clouds, Two Stones, One Willow.

The Moon was built of Rice and Wood
    And her Dresses sewn from Fountains
Hidden in the sodden Sun
    Three Roads, Two Bones, One Mountain.

The Sleeping Lake
    Inside the Sun
Inside the Moon
    A Mouse's Gun
The Moon was pink
    The Sun was blue
The Lake was bored
    The Gun was too

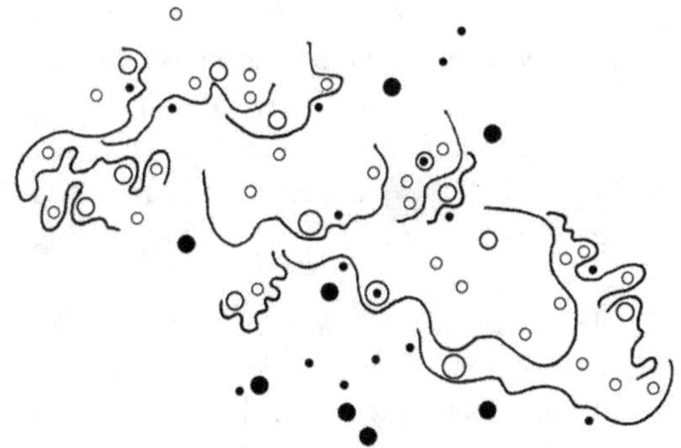

The Sky despaired of mending Love
    For either Sun or Moon
And jumped into the Sleeping Lake
    Three Rooms, Two Boats, One Spoon.

The Mediterranean Snail and The Faithless Bride

Once upon a tidy teatime in a neighborhood of quaint wig shoppes and even quainter baby brothels a wedding ceremony drew only the curious and the failed as a delicate bell tinkled beneath the Bride's veil to announce the advent of another disturbing conversation about the dark back bedroom which – but for the cultural monkey chained to the bedstead – appeared to be merely another bourgeois fantasy made real by too much money. But alas the secular humanists are not part of this tale. Let's discuss the Mediterranean Snail.

The silly parents of the silly Bride had purchased for her – from a passing drifter – a tiny infant daughter to spare her the social embarrassment of childbirth which had killed the beloved Princess Unadora, older sister and embezzler of the Bride's legacy. This young Gypsy baby had a small red snail trapped in her ear and the parents were informed – by another drifting stranger – that it was indeed a rare Mediterranean Snail. This was not totally unexpected because – in her pretty little nose – lived a Caribbean Slink and these two facial animals liked to send messages to one another via a miniature pulley system they had constructed from snail shells, slink skin, and hair from the baby's eyelashes. The Snail – an altogether suspicious sort – accused the Slink of being of New Zealand descent while the Slink for his part was convinced that the Snail's one real charm was how he rode out earthquakes with a fragile Continental *joie de vivre.* A famous Fox ran the pulley system for the two haughty facial animals and took his pay by removing some vowels from each missive and selling them to a Hedgehog in a nearby Homburg Hat full of Worker Bees. This Fox weekended in Moscow and often wiped his plate clean of honey with a slice of bread stolen from the Snail who – of course – knew nothing.

And so, a certain air of marital accord was sustained by an elaborate system of pulleys and gluttony and suspicion, freeing up a lot of government energy and finances to wage several wars in which the Bride's future husbands all died.

THE END

He Dreamt Each Night of Bethlehem

He dreamt each night of Bethlehem
Its beaches washed by Sundays
And of peaches shaped like pears
For breakfast every Monday.

He built a boat of frozen dates
And he sealed each hole with socks
So, he might sail to Bethlehem
On a Sea of Sacred Clots.

But once upon the sticky sea
A Roman waved him o'er
To tell him of kaleidoscopes
For sale on local shore.
So, like a Croesus did he spend
His time and money fled
Faith had bought him one fishwich
And a kaleidoscope made of bread.

So, dream of reaching Bethlehem
And build your leaking vessel.
You too shall seek kaleidoscopes
And be just as unsuccessful.

An Unpretentious Behavioral Thesis

Wrens & Robins
Steal Beads & Bobbins
Because they lack in Virtue.
Skinks & Scallops
On Giraffes will Gallop
On account they do prefer to.
Ruins & Rubble
Tutors & Trouble
Goddamn & Glory.
It's the end of my story.

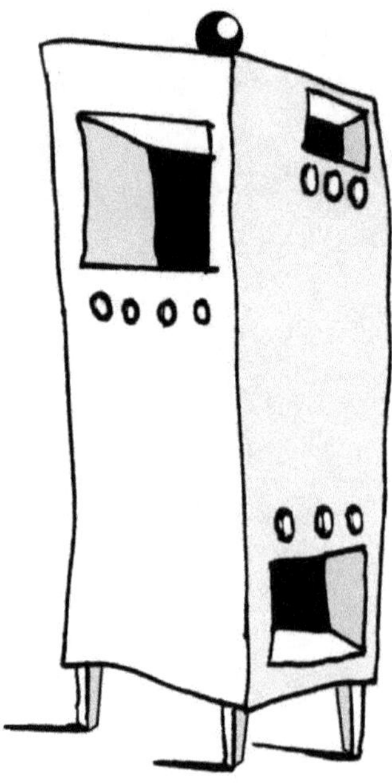

The Upstairs Horse & the Downstairs Horse

A Horse upstairs pulled a Big Wheel around in his ash tree Carriage
and waved like a Big Wheel himself to a Horse passing in the Street below
pulling a bigger Big Wheel in a smaller ash tree Carriage.
These two Horses became Lovers even though Dust floated eternally
up from the Carpet, making courtship difficult over the Years.

Escaping down the narrow Staircase the Upstairs Horse
upsets His Carriage, and a Bloody Napkin is thrown
from its Medical Berth. After Midnight
the bloody Napkin is entangled in Social Engagements.
The Downstairs Horse uses a Bloody Napkin
to predict Fires at Parties.

Sunday, the Upstairs Horse schedules a Luncheon
with the Downstairs Horse, who shall provide
a Bag of Roasted Swans & a Tureen of Swan Bisque.
With luck, the Hidden Onion will not imply Indigestion
easily killing the Horse who consumes it.

The Upstairs Horse will turn his broken Carriage Wheels
into a Crawdaddy Trap which, when set in the Window
shall catch a Breakfast for the Downstairs Horse.

The Downstairs Horse is gripped in a Crawdaddy Trap
of broken Carriage Wheels which was set in the Window
to catch a fine Breakfast for the Downstairs Horse.

The Blossom Eased Against the Pane

After a Sunset of Green Marble, the Moonrise was Grass-colored
as He had promised. He is sliding nearer You, His Back to the Moon
His Hands a Tiny Blaze. Room after Room, in the Air so Green
Room after Room, His Hands a Tiny Blaze. He is sliding nearer You
His Back to the Moon, His Hands a Tiny Blaze.

And your Eyes two torn Leaves, He circles because He is a Dog.
A Dog black behind the Dark Net of Branches strangled with Vines.
Vines into which You once dipped one tired Wing. He is sliding nearer You
His Back to the Moon, His Hands a Tiny Blaze.

You stand now in the same Room with Him, bent above the Steam Beds.
The Beauty of Green Stones lay in the second Room yet it's only a Floor.
The third is a Low-Ceilinged Maze of Trees in the Air still so Green
Room after Room, your trembling Body of almonds baked in Silver Paper.

Or trapped beneath your Clothes, Clothes of colored Grass
& Silver Paper. The Moon of colored Grass even as He promised You
sliding nearer You. His Hat casts its silly Shadow upon a Steeple Clock.
trapped beneath Your Clothes. The Steeple Clock casts its generous Shadow
upon the Garden below.

The Garden casts modest Shadow upon his House and his Hours.
Where They fall these Shadows are a Tiny Emerald Blaze, a Spark of Calyxes.
He casts His Shadow far across a Weeping Silver Woman. Nothing is stolen
save the Wilderness of her Skin.

Light's Door shut upon the Edge of Her Blossom, bolted
from the Outside. A latticed & humane Bed, dirty Yellow Bed
blown into the center of the Street. A Bed wide as a Man
and nailed shut at the very Top with her Blossoms.

I fear for that dreaded Neck beneath her Glass Head.

Her Glass Head framed against Narcissus
& Anemone & Nicotine Smoke.
He is sliding nearer You, His Back to the Moon, His Hands a Tiny Blaze
Room after Room, in the Air so Green
Room after Room, His Hands a Tiny Blaze. He is sliding nearer You
His Back to the Moon, His Hands a Tiny Blaze.

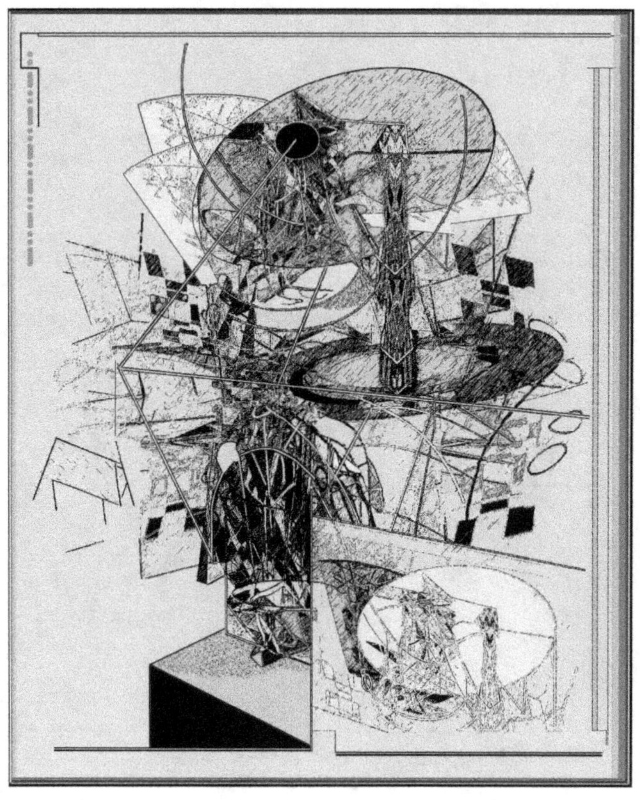

An Astonishment of Butterflies

Once upon a Choking Desire there existed our Grandmother with some biscuits in the forest you can see right over there. She took a path to a longer path and to an even longer path that led to an open door but a gruff voice (which lived in the forest you can see right over there) called out *"Who's there?"* and our Grandmother stopped and she listened for a short time that led to a longer time and to an even longer time in which butterflies having lingered far too long in that open door caught a chill and shook themselves to pieces onto a piece of bread just in time for lunch.

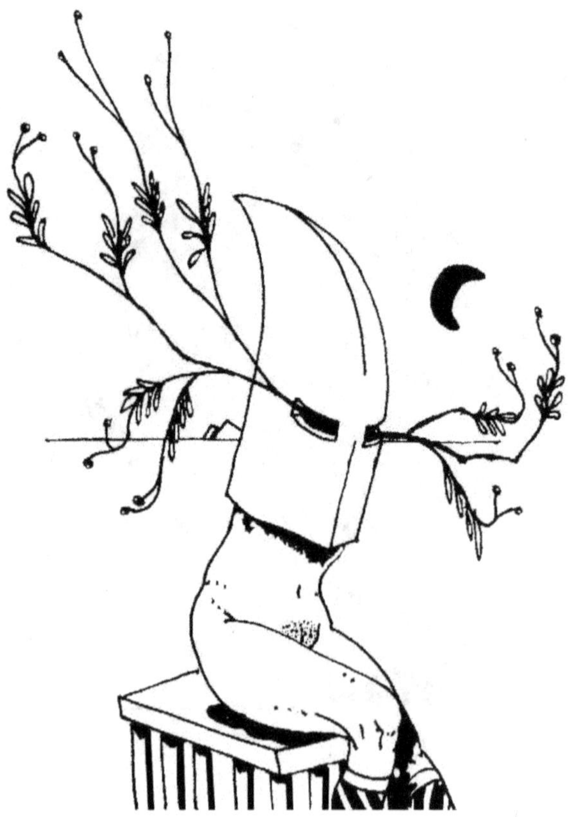

Heaven Is Still a House
dedicated to Edgar Allan Poe

A facade of frosted gargoyles cast in lime welcomed me to the house
and though intricacies of either Art or Science tend to excite
quaint animations in my usually conservative limbs, the properties
of both my Fancy and my Terror mixed to form a startling base coat.
The exterior of the box appeared too frail and I resolved
to attend to its repair at some later time. After my curiosity dimmed
and I was fallen back upon mere preservation of the structure.

A few white flakes, a pale rust fell from metal ceiling
and I resolved to attend to its repair at some later time.
The ponderous detail in these most *obtrusive* signs of Beauty
seemed to my convalescent eye to be arrayed
in distinctly *semaphoric* columns while distant *optical* panels
served to secrete a vivid passivity. I desired to reveal all *chemically*
but I believe my *physical* deficiencies are best explored
within a mesmeric laboratory.

The closer I drew to the bedroom, the more sensations
grew like gray polyps (like insect eggs) upon the high walls
and I now recalled in maddening detail the eccentric condition
of the entrance flagstones, a chitinous pulp lay between
the stones, and I had resolved to attend to its repair
at some later time. As it was a moist house and drafty
I imagined a rich proprietor of singular reserve and *presence.*

In my convalescent eye I saw his *passionate* orthodoxy
as manifest in the milky lineaments of his face, and yet still beheld
a new and strongly parallel species to mankind; this proprietor
possessed a black oaken eye that seemed to hang
upon the very air itself!

His black nostrils suffered from *encrimsoned* membranes
and I resolved to attend to its repair at some later date.
Once more certain ponderous details signaled.
My own black-breath rose was feeding the atmosphere
of this new planet; an atmosphere which -
with what horror I now recall (when I am forced to recall) -
appeared to own a sentient *countenance* which searched me out
and hungered for the sight of me!

How France Got Berets

The Flaming Red Waterfalls attracted many tramps and other men of science along with local clowns who brought hand-painted butterflies to mollify the over-excited sparrows who chattered on the riverbanks. One very important clown – Queasy Black Branches – had a tattoo of a blind swan on his/her forehead and was accompanied by three naked and great-chested men with tiny blue heads who carried huge live lobsters on their backs to sacrifice to the waterfalls which – unfortunately – had dried up beneath all the adoration leaving only the memories of a crashing upsurge gasping on the linoleum boulders. Queasy Black Branches took great umbrage and had the offending boulders flattened into sporty hats for the nearby villagers. Everyone agreed this was the finest jest of all. And so, they beat the clown to death as a punchline.

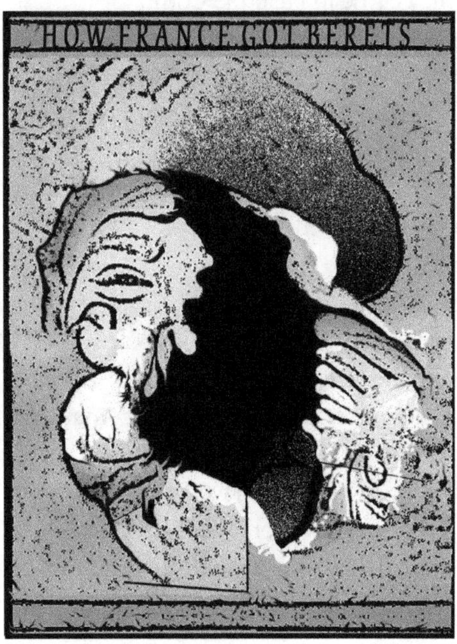

The Two Young Girls, the Coffin, and the Kettle Monkey

The Two Young Girls kissed the Coffin
beneath the Branches of the Natural Church. A Thing shuffled
across the Floor of the Natural Church & Local Tavern.
Beneath the Branches of the Natural Church & Local Tavern
a Thing shuffled.

Beneath the Natural Church & Local Tavern
Chrysanthemums in piles! And piles of Samurai Hats!
The Two Young Girls had not broken their Promise to the Samurai.
They brought a Wine made from Lemon Peel
to sprinkle upon the Road
to sprinkle upon the Road
as the coffin slid on thin tin sledges
burning.

In the end they chose to push the Coffin
down a country Road into the Main Library
and in the Library sat a rose-colored Kettle Monkey
talking to a sinister Racehorse, who soon galloped off
with the usual Kettle Monkey Teeth
who soon gnawed through the Casket Lid
and through the black shroud
with hand-detailed hot-rod flames.

Outside, a Policeman wiped his Hands
on the Branches of the Natural Church & Local Tavern.
Wiped his wet red dumb Hands upon the Two Young Girls
caught beneath the Branches, kissing the Coffin.
Down his Road every grouping of Two Young Girls pass
sticky red like everything else from the Birth Canal
of the Church & Local Tavern & Racetrack.

With his tiny Policeman Teeth
he had soon gnawed through the Casket lid
and through the black Shroud
with hand-detailed hot-rod flames.

Beneath the Branches of the Natural Church
& Local Tavern & Racetrack & Jail
those Two Splendid Young Girls
(who had not broken their Promise
to the Samurai) kissed.

Envy of the Maggot Flies

Three Mournful Moonlit Maggot Flies
Two Blue as Early Sleep
One As Red as Purple Waves

Which Gallop On the Deep.

One Cheerful as A Chim-me-ney
Two Proudly Custom-Free
Three In Later Autumn's Chill

I Envy the Honeybee.

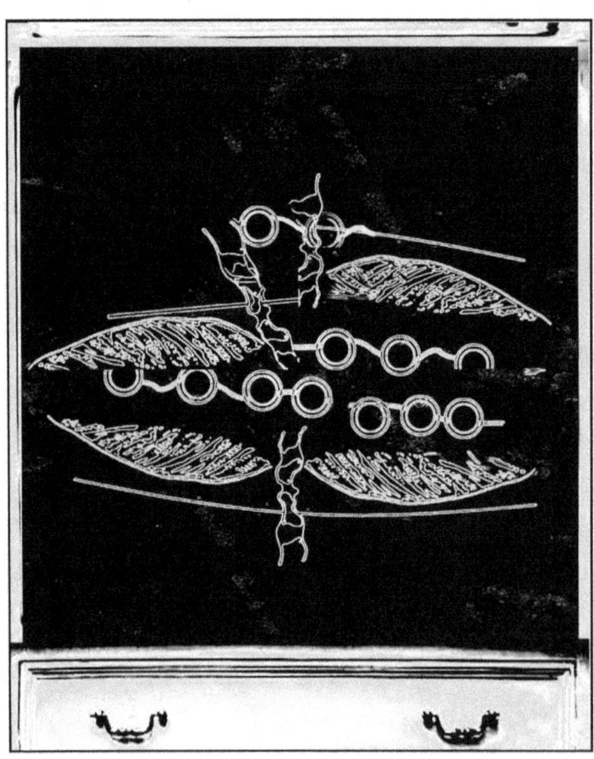

A Fable of Discrete Personality

Even Tortoise appears sufficiently swift to catch Dense Thoughts
Such as, *"Perhaps We might drink from the Cold Stream and take a Dip"*

But Hare is a surprisingly incompetent Thief
As He fails to steal even one Short Sip.

In Centuries past Tortoise tended Her Garden well
Although eventually Everyone still went Home quite famished

While Hare dreams nightly of Lettuce with Interest
Even as He rarely uses His Dreams to Practical Advantage.

Seems the phlegmatic Tortoise is fond of Grand Speeches
If simultaneously She was more enamored of a Small Silence.

All the same Hare dwells inordinately upon the subject of Laughter
Even as He rarely uses his Contemplations to Aid in His Advance.

Also, Tortoise is average quick for one with a Round Body
Yet She seldom raises either Dust or Undue Headlines.

All the same Hare remains of Scanty Build and Nervous Aspect
Often darting incautiously into Open Sacks or Poison Vines.

The Cawing Brothers

In the lettuce where we saw woods
we saw also The Cawing Brothers.

In the whispering windows
freshly broken
by the Cawing Brothers.

When done put on a gown
as the face is quietly ready
to meet The Cawing Brothers.

A tree of yellow hearts
that is night stirred
by The Cawing Brothers.

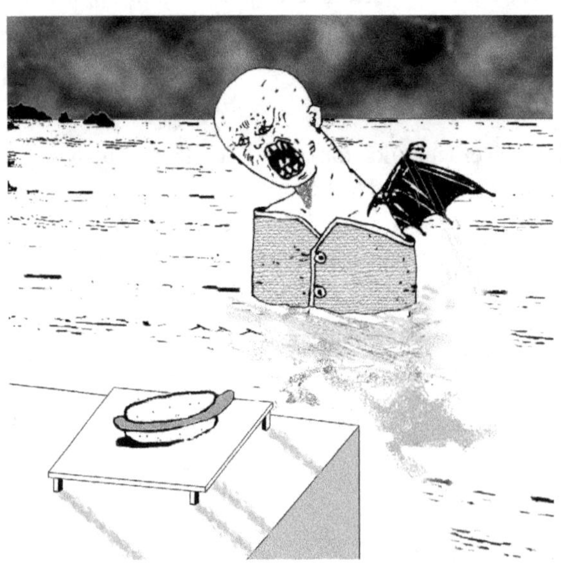

The Crow & the Entrepreneur

The Man who discovered that Crows were not cut
from Yesterday's Sky with any common Axe
because he thought to make a Decent Living
doing precisely that for the Widow Women
was disillusioned.

He had been told by a Priest moonlighting
as a Widow Woman whom he suspected of moonlighting
as a Thief and also that the Widow Women
liked their Escorts to carry Axes.
This Priest had cozied his way into their Hearts
and knew such Secrets.

The Widow Women drink scented Lily Oil
to make the Priest kiss them, and they do so love to kiss
along cold Railway Tracks, beneath the Branches
of the old Railway Maple, inside the Roundhouse.

This Railway Priest and these Railway Widow Women
were like cold Steel within the Shadow of the Crow's Nest
which blanketed the Railway Village.

Still the Railway Widow Women
measure the Hat-ribbons of the Priest
and compare the Results
to the length of their scented Lily Oil ladle
which was carved from Railway Maple.

The Man who discovered that Crows were not cut
from Yesterday's Sky with any common Axe
because he thought to make a Decent Living
doing precisely that for the Widow Women
was disillusioned.

But Not One Crow

I see the Famous Fabric Fox
Who hides behind the Wall

I see the Watercolor Wave
Which drowns the China Doll.

I see the Large and Lacquered Lynx
Stored in a tiny Box

I see a Clutch of Cloistered Clams
A Child molds into Clocks.

I see the Penguin's Plaster Pig
Who has caught the Plastic Pox

But not one Crow did I once see
Not Paper, nor Tin, nor Phlox.

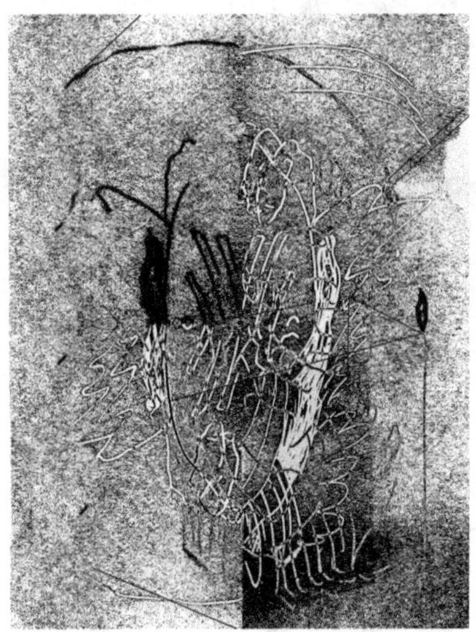

Just Yesterday

Just yesterday

1 Sparrow with Paper Wings
Was such a wondrous Thing.

Yet today

4 Whales that swim the Stars
Won't draw that much Applause.

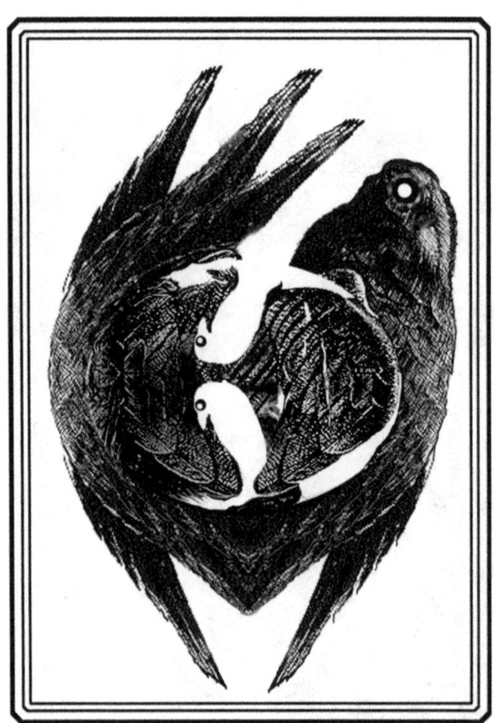

A Small Western Melodrama

On Stone you grew
old ghosts of a new Heart

& a Sun of poverty
banked in the Sky

veined Shadows
chained to the Clouds.

§

Sleep is most Misery
when Misery sits among the Missing

and the strange Toy Flame
finds a second's easy purchase

like a Wolf in the Aspens
Like a Kiss of broken Obsidian.

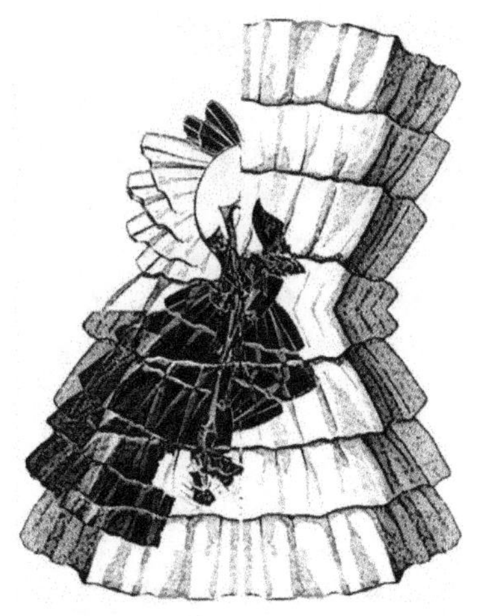

The Starlit Dog

The Starlit Dog has fallen into the River
just as he was about to open his PinkMouth
& curse his Mother.

Just as he was about to reveal his Plan
for Maturing Money in muddy times
from inside a Blue PinBox
or a DrawingRoom
with a huge FeatherBed
in the Sea.

Let us be kind to the Starlit Dog this Evening.
Let us not lose Patience with the Starlit Dog
& his Maniac WidowBees this Evening.

He sold his one SunBeam to a PaperMill
to bolster their "Executive" Stationery
and he is also that DeadSoul
who works all night in a PaperMill
and can't catch a Cut.

Don't look into his blue PinBox
slotted into the Earth with Iron Screws.
He owns a LookingGlass
which only reflects a Sow
and her Son.

The rest of the Royal Litter
don't see fit to wish him a Goodnight.
He sleeps surrounded by AppleTrees
and Children with WidowBee Eyes.

But I am losing Patience
with the Starlit Dog
and his Mad WidowBees.
Just as he was prepared
to open his PinkMouth
and curse his Mother
he fell into the River.

In Fairyland After a Recent Court Decision

The King was kinging in Dairyland.
The Queen admired the Butler's Butter
Some ugly Prince-Thing used his Hand
To slaver Soft Cheese on the Shutters.

Can You too?
You can too
Toucans who
take in the view

A small Red Tent was being painted
White to keep the Blackbirds in joy.
The Baronet's Bacon was tainted
Now his Parts are motoring in the boy.

Can You too?
You can too
Toucans who
Take in the view

"Two can play at this game," gamely
Quoth the Butter to the Butler.
"Tame the Gnu, it's so ungainly,"
Returned the Butler with a flutter.

Can You too?
You can too
Toucans who
Take in the view

Now it's quiet, much like the Ermine
Creep into the Trap and die there.
High above, the Moon's Pale Vermin
Eat the tiny Prince-Thing's Pie Square.

Can You too?
You can too
Toucans who
Take in the view

The Wondrous Tapir

Let's celebrate the Wondrous Tapir
Which I suppose looked good on Paper
Yet trans-a-lated into Flesh
His Piggy charms seem very less.

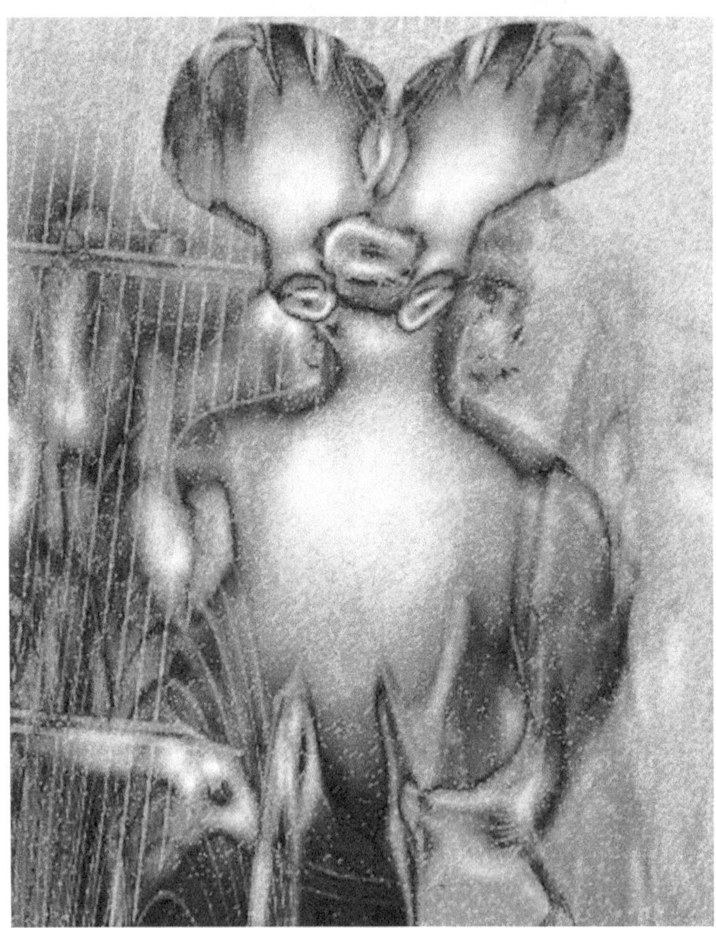

The Khan and The Squirrel Army

Once upon a time a famous Khan threw off his cloak of power and ran away because he had heard foul words spoken about his character and a great fear came over him that his people were prepared to storm his citadel and throw him to the wolves below the city walls. He took along one talking unicorn from his vast repository of marvelous beasts both because he would want someone to talk to upon the journey ahead and someone to ride swiftly away on if he ran into a Giant with big shoulders. At night he only pretended to be asleep and kept one eye upon the wild boars on the hillside.

In the morning a large chamber door had appeared in one of the hillsides and the unicorn (very bravely) suggested they should go and open it. When they did, they saw inside a vast oceanfront and a ship lying in wait for them. The Khan was very pleased for he loved to sail and so they both boarded the great ship whose hold was full of gilded trousers and jackets of a magnificent cut. The two rejoiced but only slightly as they were only trousers and jackets no matter how marvelous or how many. If they had known what else was on the ship, they might have fled but they didn't and so they didn't.

And by and by the ship mysteriously unmoored itself and took to the sea and they were prisoners if voluntary ones.

On the next day they came across a furious beast in the captain's quarters: a wild, boarish chaplain with a gaping mouth and glistening teeth. It chased them down the hallway to its little chapel where they darted in and slammed the heavy door behind them. Inside our two travelers did much damage with just as much pleasure and taunted the wild chaplain from behind the locked door, shouting that he was *"a mere nothing."* Eventually they rushed out and captured him and bound a rope around its neck, tied him to a tree growing out of the deck and chopped at him with tiny axes. The unicorn rushed with all its strength against the tree and so toppled it into the water but not without losing its golden horn which made him just another small horse after all and so of no real use to the Khan who was very demanding of animals and people. So, the Khan gathered up a little store of food and walked off into a dense forest he had seen at the stern of the ship and after several days of walking, he arrived at the outskirts of a small village which had been recently attacked by a Giant. The Khan demanded that the head of the mayor be brought to him on a silver dish, for he had begun to think more like the Khan of old than just another fugitive from the people's ire and desired once again to rule a kingdom of his own, and he knew that all kingdoms begin in small, frightened villages.

The mayor's head was delivered and then he chose the prettiest daughter from amongst the few which had been spared by the Giant (which meant she was barely bearable to look at) and married her on the spot, and so they became the Royal Family. It's that simple really.

But the unicorn (now only a small horse) had not given up on the Khan and had trailed him to the village, but not before he had come upon the Giant and made a pact with him to the effect that they would rule together over this forest if only the Giant would kill the Khan and give his not-so-pretty bride to him to be his slave. Then the Giant uprooted many trees and built a lifeboat, for he was well aware that they all were traveling on a ship and would someday need to escape. The he drew his great sword and cut a deep wound in the breast of the unicorn from which flowed a multitude of squirrels who soon filled up the clearing in which they both stood and became his army.

"I believe that I might soon die," said the wounded unicorn, *"and this is too bad for I would rather have enjoyed watching your squirrel army defeat the Khan."* And then he died and fell upon the ground where several trees instantly sprung up from his blood. Then the Giant fell upon the rest of the body and sated himself for he was very hungry and needed his strength for the battle ahead. But he found himself to be very tired from his murderous labors and so fell asleep under the beautiful new trees so filled with angry squirrel soldiers that were chattering in complaint about their wages and the food. And the shoddy housing. And the weather.

The Giant dreamed that he was a large pink stone in the middle of a river and that the branches above him shook violently since they were full of lions peering about him on all sides and speaking to him softly about the One Hundred Daughters of the Kingdom from which only one might be chosen to kiss him - and turn him into a normal man - if he defeated the Khan and became the Rightful Ruler of the small forest once more as it had been of old, for a curse had been laid upon him by a magic tailor because he had feared the other's might. Thus had a Giant been created and all the forest trembled and shook with his approach day and night. For that is the way of the Giant.

Then the Giant awoke.

At the other end of the small forest the Khan and his Bride had built a fine home near the river, and he had forgotten that he was really just on a large ship in the middle of a vast ocean floating aimlessly about the wide world. The villagers came to him when he was not asleep (which was not often these days) and begged him to cut down the trees and build lifeboats for they knew someday the ship would run aground and they would have to escape. But the Khan did not take advice from anyone but his Bride, who was not only common-looking but also stupid, and so he spent much of his waking time building more rooms onto their home until a huge chunk of the forest was used up in such nonsense, for there was no limit to the number of rooms the Bride felt were necessary and neither would believe the strange story that their forest was only a small patch of trees on a ship's deck out on a large ocean. Often the Khan was totally lost in the middle of this huge maze of chambers and was only found by great effort on the part of his servants. One day after he had journeyed some large distance in the house, he came into the courtyard of the magic tailor who had taken up residence in the mansion seeing that there was little chance of his being discovered. There the tailor being quite cheerful in his new home told the Khan the story of the cursed Giant and of his mighty squirrel army and of how only a unicorn's blood could create this vast army which so frightened the Khan (for he suddenly remembered how he had abandoned his friend) that he jumped up from the chair he was seated in and gave the tailor a death-blow which seemed a good idea at the time until - from the deep wound on the tailor's head - arose a roasted sheep who spoke to him about the struggle to come and then went to sleep in a nearby bed which was soon covered with sheep grease and quite repulsive to behold, so the Khan set fire to the bed and ran away to another room.

When midnight came and the servants still had not found him (for he was in a part of the huge house that no one ever went to except the mice) the Khan sat by the edges of the raging house fire and imagined that he saw a giant cherry-tree in the flames and - as he knew that cherries were a sign of premature death - he shook visibly at this horrible omen. So, then he decided to build himself a small lifeboat and escape from the ship if he could first escape from this house and then from the forest. Furthermore, he hoped he would someday find the chamber door again and so return to his own land for he was homesick. So, he began gathering wood and wandering about without hope in the dark hallways.

The Giant meanwhile had approached the village at the head of his mighty squirrel army and was ready to attack when three villagers

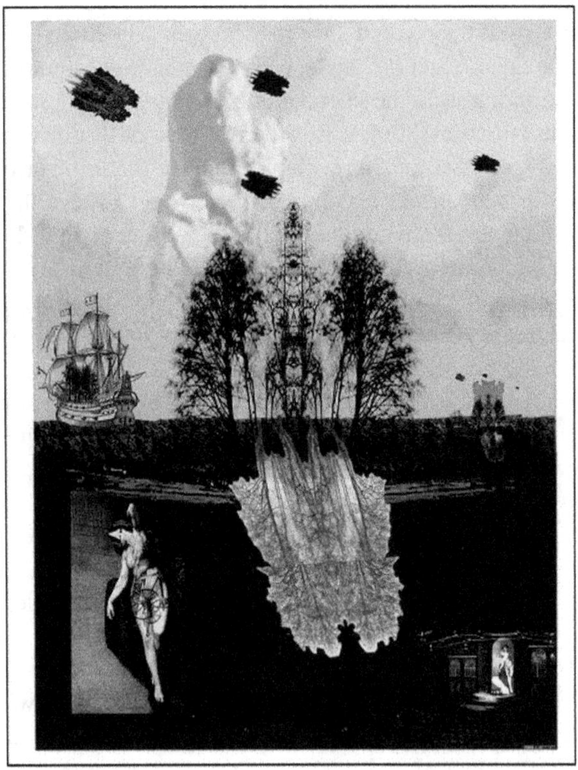

came out to him and offered to give the Khan up to his benevolence if they could only find him and thus be spared destruction for they were a cowardly lot although many of them had once been able seamen.

"With pleasure I accept your offer," roared the Giant for he was not up to the fight and only wished to crush the Khan into cherry jam and eat him upon a great slice of acorn bread such as was made by the cooks of the squirrel army. Then the cowardly villagers ran off to search for the Khan, but they were soon lost in the maze of chambers and courtyards and hallways and two of them were never seen again. The third was seen just once - at a great distance - struggling up a tree to get a clear view of his position but there is no proof that he ever did. And so ended their tale.

"Well done, as usual," said the Giant to himself as he reluctantly prepared for war.

Meanwhile the Khan's Bride had befriended a bluebird and kept it in her pocket where it stored all the little nuts and seeds it collected during the night when it flew free over the great house. One morning she noticed that one of the little nuts and seeds was a tooth and so she asked the bluebird where he had found it, thinking it might be the Khan's. When the bluebird told her the Bride sent two servants out to recover the Husband who - although he wasn't much of a companion - still had the only keys to the money room and besides was good company when he wasn't out killing the cowardly villagers and robbing them of their few possessions. While they were gone, she wondered what she might say to the Khan once they were reunited and she decided on *"There you are, you ignorant pigmy. I fancied I could have done better than you."* As I said she was not a very clever woman and barely bearable to gaze upon.

Soon they dragged the Khan (laden with a small handmade boat) back to the main chamber where the lovers pretended to be thankful for their reunion and cheese was served to everyone in the kingdom although it was not very good cheese as it was infested with flies' eggs.

At midnight as the Bride slept in the massive bed, the Khan ran away with his small boat hoping to be out of the forest by daybreak. But things don't often turn out so well for such men, and they didn't this time either, for the Giant had seen him scurrying through the woods and so hurried after him with the entire squirrel army in tow. Soon as he was within sight of the evil Khan, he drew a pebble from his pocket (which was really a large boulder) and smashed the Khan's head in with one well-aimed toss. *"You rascal! You wretched bad creature!"* He yelled at the dead man for some minutes while the squirrel army - espying the small boat - plotted to escape the ship altogether, leaving behind the depleted forest, the cowardly villagers, the not-so-pretty Bride and the not-so-clever Giant.

"We're off to seek our fortunes!" they all shouted in unison snatching up the small lifeboat and heading toward the ship which was now quite visible through the dis-arbored forest. The Giant was busy picking tiny pieces of old cheese from the Khan's body and so did not notice he had been abandoned by his squirrel army who were making ready to travel forth into the wide world.

The Bride's bluebird meanwhile had become lodged in a dense bush and died which so upset the Bride she bound a belt about a tree and hanged herself.

The army finally made it to the ship's deck and threw the lifeboat over the side and leapt in. There were also a great number of flies aboard as the squirrels were not as clean as they might be and the small particles of bad cheese in their fur had harbored many a fly egg.

Then they sailed until they found the chamber door and entered through to the Khan's homeland.

And that is how so many trees have so many high-spirited squirrels in them.

THE END OF MY SQUIRREL'S TAIL

His Heels Went to War with His Soul Over a Gas-Powered Hurdy Gurdy

His Heels went to War with his Soul
over a Gas-powered Hurdy Gurdy.
From beyond the dark Dwarf Cannons
emerged a Thrush and at the Dawn
all varieties of Misspeakings.

This Affair was of no social Use
to anyone, save the Papers
and his Heels assured us
they remained loyal
to German Girls in German Cars.

The Soul's Axle was ornamentally padded
in blood-red Velveteen, and its Black Heels
lay in Pink Wooden Cages
and were fed on Chalk.

The Thrush meanwhile is dignified
perched upon a Palm Tree
on Wheels behind the Sofa
while the Heels escaped
(with the aid of Two Magpies)
to whip its Soul with long Laces.

It was all quite unseemly
till we turned to face the Gas-powered Hurdy Gurdy
as socially useful as a White Cat's Reflection
in as Puddle of warm Milk.

From beyond the dark Dwarf Cannons
emerged a Thrush, dignified & perched.
About the Sofa totter Calves
with Lemon Yellow Mustachios
like Diplomats.

We try and yet fail to admire
their Gelatinous Moon Ray
fallen upon a Mummy,
whose Genital-Blue Balalaika
sings of Wartime Roses.
The Soul's Axle was ornamentally padded
in blood-red Velveteen, but we kindle
one dry Conversation
by admiring its slender laced Waist.

We try and yet fail to admire
its Ossified Moon Ray fallen upon a Mummy.
It was all quite unseemly
till we turned to face the Gas-powered Hurdy Gurdy.

And the Thrush remains as a Policeman
disguised as Two Young Dancing Girls
and his Campaign is a tragic Misfortune
for the Birds & the Wartime Roses
& the Mummy.

But you see, don't you see,
don't you see? This Affair
was of no social Use
to anyone, except the Papers.

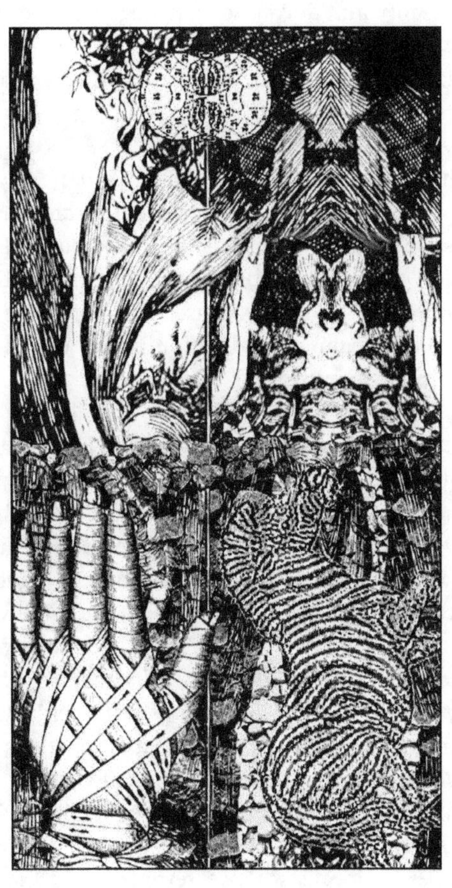

After the Simple Wars

After the Simple Wars many splendid funeral feasts were held, with some lasting an entire week, which was very pleasing to Queen Perforation whose efficient vanity and devout love of degenerate luxury was known to all her subjects and publicly applauded to avoid extermination. She owned five platinum carriages, a *"poverty holiday"* walkup in the quaint village of Stane-on-Westcutt, and hundreds of little service boys dressed up as soldiers who were fated to die in the next series of wars she loved to have with neighboring countries who had never done anything to her but ruin her view of the sea with their church spires and castles, which was not very aggressive of them when one thinks about it. But let's not. But Queen Perforation enjoyed dreaming of the slaughter and so many of her people suffered because – well - because. Such things will happen and is it not our duty to bear pain and daily humiliation with a smile? Many of us think so. Or think we must think so.

King Perforation XIII was meanwhile hanging by his ankles in the main root cellar for he was a perturbation to the Queen who had always believed that he should be grandiose and opulent rather than merely benevolent. But even the adorable daydreams about his suffering had begun to bore her so she sent word all through her kingdom of her desire to attend some diverting entertainment that didn't involve the King's humiliating position. So, several of her more loyal followers hurried into their wagons and set out to find some amusements for their Queen. In short time they had discovered three dogs who could whistle operettas through their fingers and a huge copper statue of a nose and a few odd slivers of something the local townsfolk claimed were once parts of a magic millhouse that could turn petty thieves (or just passing strangers) into a nutritious flour from which they made their famous Pretty People Cakes. The scarpering loyalists hoped (even beyond the question of the Queen's being difficult to distract from hangings and decapitations) that this last item at least would stop their ruler from having them hanged for they were selfish and valued their small existences. So it goes with such delicate solipsists. We who are brave in the face of our degradation revile them!

Yet the dogs failed to whistle on command and were gutted with a rusty brooch - which made it much more unlikely that they would perform magnanimously in the future. The copper nose began to run, and repulsed the Queen and was quickly melted down for pots and pans. Worst of all the broken shards turned out to be merely the remnants of an alehouse drain pipe. Her Insufferable Highness was both mortified and (as expected) furious, and so ordered the would-be entertainment-providers to be hung up next to the King who rather relished the thought of company to the point that his eyes grew as large as serving platters although they remained empty of any nourishment for the Queen. For this impertinence his most precious spouse had him beaten with a newly forged copper pot and (for good measure) tossed the entire royal council into the sea although she could not see this because of all the intervening church spires and castles. Several thousand people watched this display of temper and found it common and intensely ho-hum. Such things will happen, and is it not our pleasure to be crushed beneath barrels of pickles with a heart full of Germanic lieder? Many of us think so. Or think we must think so.

Next a soldier (named Fetcher Juggle) stepped forth and boasted to the Queen that he would ride out into the greater world returning with a marvel that would stagger even her Blessed Gratuitousness. He tied an opportunity ladder upon his nag, Yokel's Heart, and rode away to the dismal fanfare of a single bent trumpet for all the other heralds had been

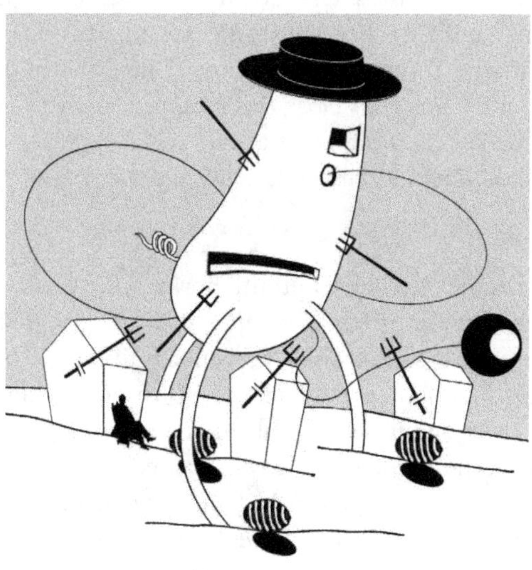

burnt at the stake for wrong notes. But the intrepid cavalier was - in fact - merely a shoemaker and he was only putting his best foot forward in his very best shoes hoping to gain a little favorable traction in the eyes of his Overripe Ruler. It was a big mistake but a well-intended one which is not to be sniffed at in an age of ill-intended mistakes.

Oh, how dark and disagreeable were the inns that Fetcher Juggle passed by with alarm drums beating in the hot air and phalanxes of marching feet hidden off behind the hedgerows and all the women wearing greasy leather aprons and shoddy slippers as they leant in their shadowed doorways, with decrepit mothers standing where only crispy fresh daughters stood a short time back. Once he looked through the iron grating of a stone prison and saw two pigs struggling inside a bag until a pair of magic jade scissors refashioned them into a petite corset. *"So that is how corsets are born and what a diverting surprise,"* he thought to himself. Still, he felt that even this would not be amusement enough for his Dark Gloriosity who had once seen a square of night-colored silk re-cut into a villager's wife. *"So that is how wives are born, and what a diverting surprise,"* she had thought to herself and promptly fallen into a boredom deeper than before. Many people died that night. Another common sight.

And so he rode on, passing doors marked with chalk scribblings of tiny birds in unique postures. The shoemaker longed for a door unmarked with a tiny bird and then he went to sleep while his horse carried him deep into the Kissoff Forest where there were no doors and thus no chalk birds upon doors. *"This is as close to Heaven as many of us are likely to get,"* the shoemaker thought. Such things will happen and is it not our fate to be pushed down a dark hole with a giggle in our throats? Many of us think so.

In the morning Fetcher's faithful horse had disappeared and the shoemaker's eyes were as big as copper pots (or pans) for he thought this very strange and so on. Thus, he walked all day through the forest and then it was midnight, so he took out his tin teacup and sat down on a wet hillside to enjoy himself, for his life had been a very laborious one up until then and he needed a little rest. Just before he fell asleep a large eagle appeared before him and asked him where his horse had gotten to. The shoemaker answered that he felt it must have been stolen, for he had tied it tightly to a small tower from which an odorous liquid seeped.

The large bird thought it likely and then struck a light to better see the shoemaker's face for he was a curious beast although quite beautiful after the foreign fashion.

After staring at the shoemaker (who was quite ugly after the foreign fashion) the bird opened his cavernous craw and spewed out a set of fine (if somewhat thickly moist) clothes which he told the shoemaker to put on. When he had done this the eagle instructed him to get on his back and he would take him to an elegant room up in the clouds where he would also be reunited with his mount, Yokels Heart. The shoemaker was dismayed to discover that this was a lie, for the eagle carried him high into the mountains and tied him to a lone tree in the center of a barren rock field where he left him to bemoan a wasted life and a bad ending and such and such. Each night sparks flew down from the leaves above his head and set fire to his fine (and now completely dry) set of clothes until he was quite naked. Thus is vanity a fleeting thing. And every morning the shoemaker (being talented and resourceful) sewed together a new set of clothes from the leaves above his head until he looked like a forest elf. Thus did many months go by.

One night (just before the sparks were about to start raining down on him) a yellow witch appeared and gave Fetcher Juggle a tinderbox saying *"I am now your only true friend. Strike this tinderbox with your needle and you will be set free."* So he did and a huge obsidian stairway appeared

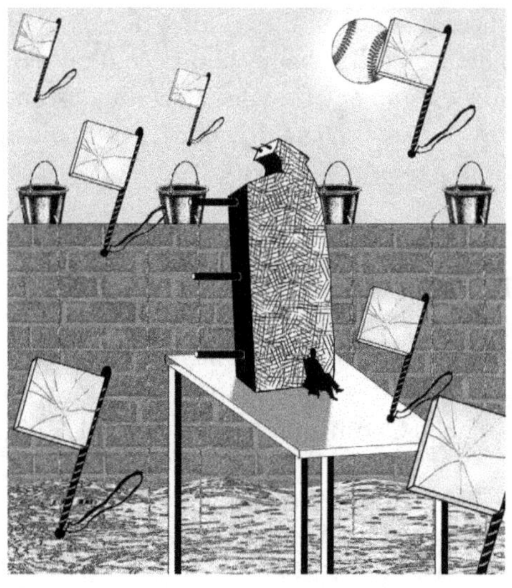

in the distance, up which he ran, anxious to escape imprisonment even if he was only to run into a different set of dangers. At the top he found himself standing in a garden, and decided it would be a relaxation to attend the garden theatre which was showing a play entitled *"A Little Money Goes Nowhere"* which bored him greatly. However, the role of the Pleasant Gentleman was played by the very eagle who had kidnapped him, so he schemed to avenge himself upon his persecutor. He made his way to the backstage door and waited there with a well-made boot in his hand. Everybody knows you shouldn't cross a shoemaker. Well, many of us think so. His own boots were now mending themselves in a garret and all for the price of only two shillings, which bankrupted the poor villagers for miles around. Many of his friends had once had fine clothes but none had owned a pair of fine boots.

Meantime the Pendant King was having a fine old time imagining that he was seated in an ostentatious hippodrome by the side of a river that flowed from the highest window of a castle in which his once beautiful daughter was cleaning his boots with a tinderbox made from a melted trumpet. While he was thus dreaming of a wonderful night of horse racing distraction a yellow witch appeared in his cell and cut off his head with a golden pocket watch after whipping him for several years with a rocking-horse tail. Gold coins fell from his open eyes. *"Good morning!"* said the yellow witch and turned into the Repugnant Queen who now had wheels that were tiny heads attached to her heels. Realizing that her easygoing spouse was now a part of the *"greater company"* she threw away the golden coins and kept the rocking-horse tail for remembrance. Then she closed his eyes with a happy chortle and put on a greasy leather apron so she could walk among the villagers without seeming too splendid. It worked for she was never splendid again. Teacups and a hundred lamps were growing from a tree.

"Not a truly horrible tale," thought Fetcher Juggle but just then the large eagle reappeared and took him off to a tea party in the hollow of a tree which grew from the Thundering Queen's forehead. He had been to the wars and now he was returning home.

All this amused the Queen and she thus repaid him with a small chalk bird.

That courtesy ends the tale.

The Red Hook

A decent Distribution System would be a good beginning to a Wedding"
thought the Panther as he penetrated the Church Girl's Defenses.
"Nothing's better than telling the Old Bones to get lost,
and Rifles don't care and eventually they will wear."

The Church Girl alone on her Porch
had once been a local Panther Priestess
and there sleeping still upon her Chest
was a Baby Panther, where her Bible
used to hang upon a Red Hook.

The Church Girl continued stealing & selling Rifles,
stealing & selling Apples, but she dreams of the Panther
breathing deeply halfway up the Apple Tree,
his warm Breath moving the Leaves.

A Panther is singing out there in the Apple Blossoms
at the very Top of the Tree. The Panther worries an Apple
out from the corner of the Church Girl's Eye
and penetrates its Defenses.

"Nothing is better than telling the Old Bones to get lost
and the Rifles don't care and eventually they will wear"
said the Church Girl as she carried an Apple across her Porch
breathing in the Scent of the Apples and the Panther.
And there sleeping still upon her Chest
was a Baby Panther where her Bible
used to hang upon a Red Hook.

The Panther retired to Country Airs
and simultaneously removed the Apples and now
the Panther didn't need to hurry
towards that distant Porch. It was now an Apple Tree
and so very still, though the Leaves were moving yet.

If All Our Pigs Were Pink Windflowers

If all our Pigs were pink Windflowers
Sing Honeysuckle Daisy and Mums
The Sea would be lit up with Candles
And the Sun would be planted with Plums.

But all our Pigs aren't Windflowers
Neither pink nor orange nor clear
While the Sea is as small as a Henhouse
And the Sun stores its Windflowers there.

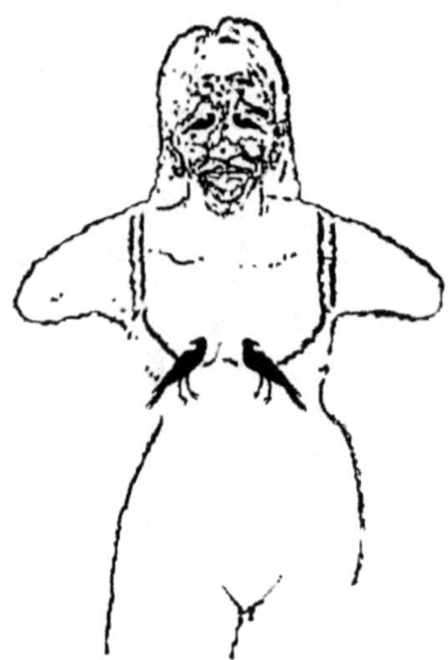

Near the Public Water Box

The Little Thug's Mind is a Public Chocolate Grinder
that sits near the Public Water Box as the Little Thug's Daughter
leans forward in her Seat.

Tiny Moonlit Cages were built for his Daughter in his Mind, and his mind
is like a Public Chocolate Grinder upholstered in RoseLeaf Lions.

In a Cloud of RoseLeaf Lions, the Little Thug's Chocolate Cot floats
and the Red Leather Pillows are Burnt NightFlowers in Tidy Moonlit Cages.

Lost in the Little Thug's mind, his Public Daughter adjusts the Pillows
while a RoseLeaf Lion is kissing the Little Thug's Daughter
upon her Back's White Chocolate.

The Little Thug's Daughter was also a Public Chocolate Grinder
that sits near the Public Water Box.
She had fashioned herself to have neither Door nor Stair.

After the White Chocolate softens in the Public Sun
the RoseLeaf Lions grow fond of her Lemon Eyes
but rushing to lick her Lemon Eyes they fall
upon the Public Chocolate Grinder
like Moon Rays long enough to be a Dress for the Little Thug's Daughter.

She is fallen upon by the Bloody Great Wolf
in his Public Armchair, dreaming.
The RoseLeaf Lions become the new Public Chocolate Grinders
grinding only White Chocolate in Moon Rays
long enough to be a Dress for the Little Thug's Daughter.

In her Lemon Eyes, The RoseLeaf Lions. The RoseLeaf Lions' Minds
are Public Chocolate Grinders and in a Cloud of RoseLeaf Thugs
the RoseLeaf Lions' Chocolate Cot floats, and the Red Leather Pillows
are Burnt NightFlowers in Tidy Moonlit Cages
where the Little Thug is busy kissing the RoseLeaf Lion's Daughter
upon her Back's White Chocolate.

A Conduct Manual for Aspiring Young Ruffians

Be sensibly post-awkward
anywhere Good Company recovers itself
too quickly to render a Profit from
and distinguish yourself from Trousers.
In accomplishing that which is most accidentally desired
varieties of ancient trick Gestures
will proof you against the vague Stumble.
Hold your butcher Knife as a grapefruit Spoon
and carve the Good Company a Taste of themselves
while ridiculously smiling
to both tire and puzzle them.
This is not improper, although it may
(given the time of Day)
reflect upon your Appellations.
To be rash is yet a Fashion of Modesty
if you can avoid the Strange Singularity
and the *"Temple of Imprudence."*
Be shocking but well-bred when spoken to
by a false-bottomed or anonymous Mate
who shall be best considered
as an Intruder
even when serving Refreshments
and especially when Dancing
and acting the *"filial Sunshine"*
which only tends to degrade
all respectable and earned Impatience.
Above all be bewildering
to the Upper-Classes
for they are of little Consequence
and usually bankroll Penitentiaries
and cannot be counted amongst your Allies.

Heart-of-Sand

The Wood waited
for you, dear Heart-of-Sand
at its Little Distance.

A Little Distance
is only a Little Dream
no longer where you left it.

The Wood waited
for you, dear Heart-of-Sand
at its Little Distance.

There is a Diamond Apple Tree
whose Seeds are the Sun
& the Moon.

When you return
awake out of the Wood,
dear Heart-of-Sand.

Fetch your Axe
in your Little Dream
of pursuing Feet.

Sleep is a Handsome Phantom
always gnawing
at the Woman's Heart.

You are a Crow
hidden in White Branches,
dear Heart-of-Sand.

The Phantom's Skin steams
one Lotus Leaf
upon a small Stove.

The small Stove
is balanced upon
one Lotus Leaf.

One Lotus Leaf
waits for you, dear Heart-of-Sand
at its Little Distance.

Sleep is a Handsome Phantom
always gnawing
at the Woman's Heart.

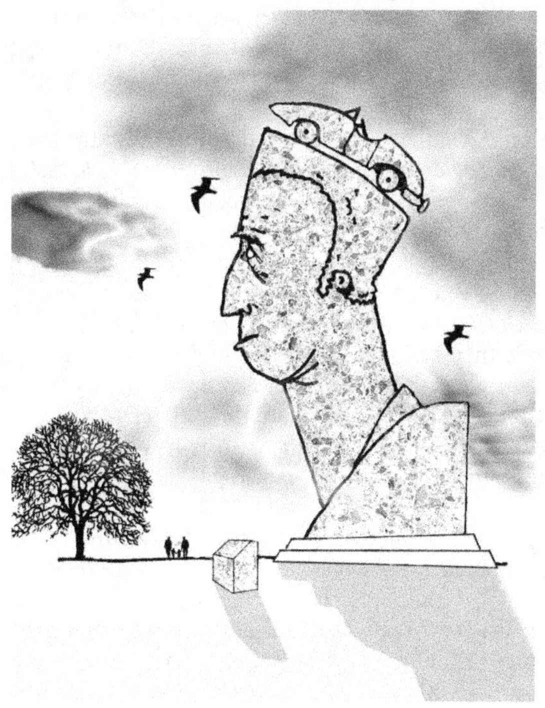

The Rapacious Tree-Child

The Shopkeeper was happy and contented as he led his new Bride, *Rape Seed,* to his tiny shop where he was joyfully received by his workers who were deathly afraid of him. It was a marvelous occasion, and the future looked bright for certain (although not many) people.

Yet - each night in the tiny cold bedroom - the woman wept. Finally, two of her tears gained voices: one that of a girl and one that of a boy, and they told her (in small wet words) that they were the wandering souls of her two younger siblings whose bodies lived in wretchedness in a faraway desert, and who ate nothing but roots and dust, and cried because they were separated from their dear sister. So, *Rape Seed* resolved to escape from this life of dull commerce, and wander about the desert until she could find them and thus regain some joy.

Then *Rape Seed* turned to the house cat who was in reality a djinn, and he told her to let down her own hair into the muddy street below and then climb down it to freedom. So, she let down her hair (which was easy for she had long golden tresses) and then climbed down it (which was difficult, but she was a resourceful beauty) and when she had reached the stones below, she cut off her locks and hung them from a hook in the window. Then she went searching for the desert.

"Ah, you stupid child!" cried the cat-djinn as they strolled along *"for you might have needed that hair to climb up something later."* They then agreed that the cat would keep its own counsel until it was asked for, and then Rape Seed wove a ladder from the cat's fur just to show herself that she was not entirely lacking in imagination and used that ladder to climb upon a giant red horse that waited outside the village's gates. The horse, named *Get Down,* was so handsome that *Rape Seed* assented to marry him once they had found her lost siblings, and freed them from the terrible desert, and in general spoke to the huge beast as though he were an old friend. They rode for many miles over rough ground until the horse grew tired then he used the cat fur ladder to climb up into a great tree where they fell asleep for the night.

When it had grown very dark, *Rape Seed* unwound the ladder and made a wig for herself for she was now entirely bald. And the cat/djinn awoke and said, *"Ah! you stupid child! What will you now use to climb out of this great tree with for you have ruined the ladder and only to satisfy your own vanity."* They then agreed (again) that the cat would keep its own counsel until it was asked for, and so they went to bed.

And that was the end of the first day.

When the cat awoke, *Rape Seed* was standing behind one of the large limbs of the great tree listening to the leaves singing about her home. Which was so charming that he stood quite still (though perched upon *Get Down*) and watched, and this was the song that the tiny leaves sang:

"Through the forest
To the tower
There's the door
Of solitude.
Unfasten the lock
But watch the hour
For here come the armies
Of disquietude."

Well... stupid enough you'll agree but the cat (although now quite hairless) was moved by the plaintive chant and climbed over to be with its mistress. It was then that the cat noticed a window set into one of the grand limbs far above their heads, and a small white figure leaning out over them. Taking some stairs that mysteriously appeared before her feet the cat ascended to the portal until it came face-to-face with the most beautiful child under the sun.

"Hello, what is your name and how might we assist you?" asked the naked cat. But the little child only went on crying, saying that there was no door in her room so that she might escape her lonely fate. The cat's heart (usually a flinty thing) was softened by the poor child's lament and so he helped her climb through the window on his tail and onto the limb where they could both descend to *Get Down* and *Rape Seed.* Then using the hair from the giant horse's magnificent tail, they fashioned a pulley to lower each and all to the ground which was littered with small pieces of red crockery.

But the child - having been so long in her prison - was terribly afraid of the wide world and hid behind the giant horse so that both the cat and *Rape Seed* (looking rather hideous in her odd cat wig) had to make her a salad from the surrounding vegetation in hopes of comforting her. It tasted so good to her that she then longed for three times as much and so they wasted the entire day (and much of the night) feeding the dear orphan until she was a large as the giant horse which so disgusted them all that they fled from her and into the forest to hide.

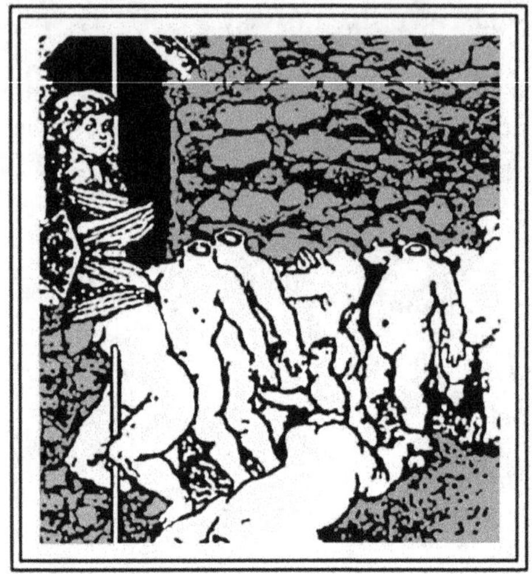

And that was the end of the second day.

The next day as they rode along toward the desert they were followed constantly by the huge child (who was unusually swift for such a huge person) who kept begging for more salad at the top of her voice and soon the trio looked quite pale and miserable, for they knew that they had no more of it to give even if they had wanted to which they didn't.

Then they came to the desert (a desert dreaded by all the world) but no one dared go into it because it was surrounded by a great wall made of snakeskin and even God avoided the place. They sat down at the very edge of the sands and fell to wishing vainly for surcease while the agonized voices of the lost siblings hung in the air and the rapacious tree-child (who was now as large as the tree she had been imprisoned in) kept on screaming at them for more salad.

And thus ends the tale. And not a minute too soon.

I Want to Be a Palm Tree

I want to be a Palm Tree
Pinned upon a Sunday Beach.
Out of breath and late for tea
Bereft of Pear nor Peach.

I want to be the Loose Tea Sea
In the Sky with Diamond Stalks.
A Roman Boat in Graecian Blood
Mooned by Scalloped Clocks.

I want a Black Onassis.
I want a Pink Kazoo
To sit upon a Pale Molasses
But to know that it's just Glue.

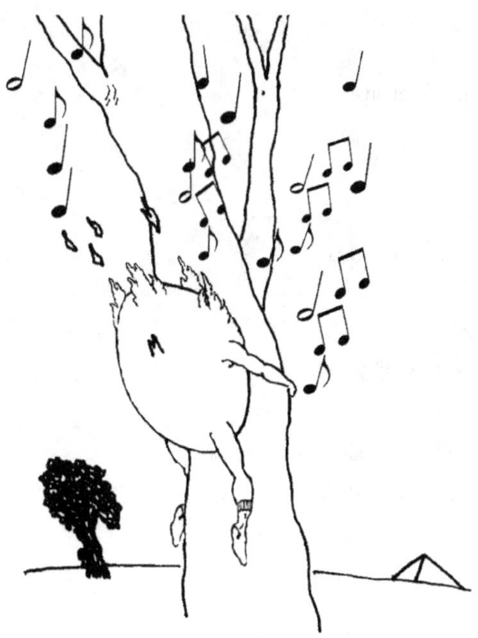

Let Them Eat Cake!

The Window made of Cake!
The Hills made of Cake!

The Two Young Girls,
the Crutches, the Trees made of Cake!

This Man's Heart a Slice of Bread
and the Good Lord a Wheaten Biscuit.

But the Birds & all the Dead People?
All made of Cake.

Her Little Cake Knife
began to drift up the Path
towards the Birds.

The Birds brilliantly lit
by the Quicksilver Lamps
dangling down their Sides.

Death is not made of Rose Leaves alas.
Death is made of Cake alas.

Quicksilver Lamps
dangling down their Sides.

Death is not made of Rose Leaves alas.
Death is made of Cake alas.

A Small Piece of Grey Cake

There was a Boy who sneered
at a small piece of Grey Cake.
at the small Grey Woods.
There was a small piece of Grey Cake
in the small Grey Woods.
The Boy sneered.

The Boy found the small piece of Grey Cake.
The small piece of Grey Cake
in the small Grey Woods.
The Boy sneered at the small piece of Grey Cake
as he sneered at the small Grey Woods.
The Boy had a small Grey Sister.

The small Gray Sister loved the small piece of Grey Cake.
The small piece of Grey Cake
in the small Grey Woods.
The Boy sneered at his small Grey Sister
as he sneered at the small piece of Grey Cake.
The small Grey sister owned a small Grey Sparrow.

The small Grey Sparrow ate the small piece of Grey Cake.
The small piece of Grey Cake
in the small Grey Woods.
The Boy sneered at the small Grey Sparrow.
The small Grey Sparrow loved the small Grey Sister.
The small Grey Sister loved the small piece of Grey Cake.

The small Grey Woods loved the small Grey Sister.
The small Grey Sister
who loved the small piece of Grey Cake.
There was no small piece of Grey Cake in the small Grey Woods.
The small Grey Sparrow ate the small piece of Grey Cake.
The Boy sneered.

The Brilliant Negligée

Once upon a Time
there was a Windowpane
sitting up in Bed drinking Cocoa
through a Porcupine Quill
which was all the Rage
in the Last Century.

The Windowpane
lacked a Convincing Cravat
if you can imagine that.
He didn't want to dress up
to go Upstairs
to the Farmland
behind the White Cooler.

The Windowpane's Brain
was one Cow dipped in Gravy
on the Farmland
behind the White Cooler.

The Windowpane dreamt
of joining a School of Fish in the Sea
because he was transparent too.

Closing his Eye, the Pane dreamed
of opening his Eye in a Seaside Cottage.
It was always getting darker
though not dark enough.

The Windowpane's Sky
was Chalk and Charcoal
in a Brilliant Negligée.
It was always getting darker
though not dark enough.

The Ebony Window-Frame

The comely hog monger's daughter named *Wire Reins* had been dead a long time while her old lover *The Great Prude* lived and reigned happily even though he had heard tell of this. Eventually - although he strained not to be sentimental - he could not help setting out to see the body as his envy of other tourists, and that his morbid curiosity was so powerful. When he arrived and saw that it was actually *Wire Reins'* old enemy, *The Glasgow Queen,* who was laid out in the plastic coffin, a feast was called for though he felt some vague unease as was usual.

On the evening of the Pseudo-Funeral Feast *The Great Prude* dressed himself and his horse in fine rich linens and gloves then gazed into an obsidian mirror and asked, *"Tell me mirror, who should I invite?"* The mirror consented to a strange list: a piece of old apple, a penniless lace factory worker named *Pity-On-Him,* a plastic coffin-maker from the inner city, several hundred carved ebony window-frames, a dove with rosy cheeks, and an owl who washed his face with wine. But it was too late to change plans, and every other bird attended also and several of them proposed to the corpse - still quite beautiful in death - sending it exquisite epistles with golden lettering, and then they all worked together and flew the coffin to the top of a hill when night came so they could comb her hair looking for bird seed. For it has always been true that bird seed was more important than love.

Could it be that her heart was still beating? For her cheeks were like small apples floating in cream. *Wire Reins* herself was nowhere to be seen but the penniless lace factory worker could refrain no longer and told *The Great Prude* that his beloved had - many months hence - gone into a secret distant tower, put her head out of a high ebony window-frame, and called to another hog-monger's daughter who was passing by the tower on the flinty pathway below, *"If it costs me my life I shall not let anyone in for I am very tempting."* But the hog-monger's daughter - poisoned by the trials of the outside world - pretended not to hear her and hurried home. Then *Wire Reins* sat down in a pile of dirty laces and began to cry.

Upon hearing this pathetic tale from the lace factory-worker *The Great Prude* went once more to his mirror and asked,

"Tremble with rage
The comb in a cage:
Where is the poison
I call Wire Reins?"

But the cloudy mirror only answered

"Good luck and good lie
A lace factory worker in the pie:
Maybe she will return
Or maybe not."

In the small village nearby there was pretty little girl with antimony hair and she traveled to the lace factory-worker's cottage to offer some for *The Great Prude* to eat. For it was well-known he had exotic tastes having been born in France. *"Fine wares to sell!"* she shouted as she passed the lace factory worker's cottage which was altogether different from the ones she had seen before due to its abundance of ebony window-frames. *"I dare not let anyone in,"* mumbled *The Great Prude* who was also little and pretty but also altogether different from the other prudes she had seen before, for he had blue shadows in his eyes. Then the blood of the pretty little girl flowed out of her ears and dressed itself up as *Wire Reins* and went to the murky mirror and spoke to it, but it replied in the same words as before and so she went home and soon came to herself again beneath the calming influence of two very brutal parents. But she wasn't through with *The Great Prude* yet for whoever is really.

In the evening the lace factory worker returned from the lace factory and was very grieved to see that *The Great Prude* was experiencing a shortness of breath and could not leave that night as he would then have to put up with him for a little while longer. *The Great Prude* told him the story of the pretty little girl and was informed by the lace factory worker that she was *The Evil Bobbin Wife* in disguise trying to trap him with her spiteful mischief. *The Great Prude* looked out of the window and past the rickety gate and over the tiny river and over the off-white hills and to the garden where he thought a bear lived, but he was much alarmed for there was no bear to be seen and he thought it may have been betrayed by one of its many servants who seldom spoke the truth, who were known scallywags and were far more beautiful than the bear itself, who looked like a peddler woman wrapped in a horse blanket. And then the muddy mirror said,

"Thou art a shaded mountain
A handsome cook, a fountain:
Wire Reins is seeking silver."

The lace factory worker pitied *The Great Prude* who was delighted to be merely lovely and so the lace factory worker went to sleep overnight with the distant bear (for they secretly loved one another). taking along a magic lamp that also served as a wonderful bed, a box to keep bread fresh in and a soothing headrest. Meanwhile *The Great Prude* began to drink wine and break plates against a wooden stool and went digging for three tiny imaginary beds hidden in the mountains, for he was certain that one of those would be too long and one would be too short and the other would be made of broken glass. And why not, after all? The world had sadness enough to fill up the days.

Near the lace factory worker's cottage *The Great Prude* stopped to pick a flower, for he was exceedingly hungry. Beyond the pathway he saw seven little glass tumblers with seven little cottages in them and so laid down to rest, for his weary feet were roaring like wild beasts and a *"peur tremblant"* left him feeling quite alone in the great forest. He dreamt of some huge creatures tearing *Wire Reins* to pieces and it melted his heart when she begged them to stop, for he was afraid that they would. Then the pretty little girl wandered by, pale with rage and envy, for she felt she was lovelier than *Wire Reins*, as bright as a seven-year-old obsidian mirror and that she should be *The Great Prude's Wife.* But she died. And turned into an ebony window-frame because Fate had a way about him.

When *The Great Prude* awoke the once-pretty little girl (and now an ebony window-frame) had grown up into a dark house in the snow and he noticed it had shed three drops of blood onto the ground which he contemplated until the flakes of snow stopped falling about him and he turned into an ebony window-frame which we can still see today in the woods outside Glasgow looking out on nothing in particular.

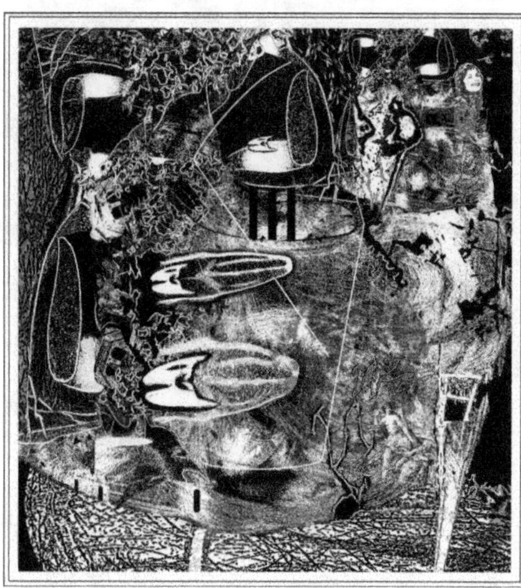

The King Became a Cat

The King became a Cat
And so, he went off to Bed
At the bottom of a Precipice
Which was his lovely Spouse's head.

And then they both became an Opera Door
Through which the Mules entered.

Snuff all your Candles
In a Basket of Pears
For the King is to marry
The Scullery Stairs

Then the Mules were loaded with Snow
When a sudden growl was heard
It was the King flying over the Stove
For the Cat had become a Bird.

And his Wife had become A Stove
Which was then buried in the Snow.

Snuff all your Candles
In a Basket of Pears
For the King is to Marry
The Scullery Stairs

The Clock Had Not Yet Struck Her Prettiest Distance

The 100 Emperors set forth
from 100 Castles all at once.

100 Apples fell into their open Hands
all at once.

It was Night inside the Apples
and the Stars joined in Drinking.

The Stars were Unionized
into one Beautiful Woman.

This one Beautiful Woman
floated above 100 Apple Trees all at once.

100 Emperors fell
into her Hands all at once.

The Clock has not yet struck
its Prettiest Distance.

Her Face's White Apple
shadowed our Little Village.

Setting forth, the 100 Emperors' Hands
fell into a Bottomless Lake.

The Bottomless Lake
became a Topless Gown.

The 100 Emperors had fallen asleep
while chasing Pebbles they dreamed were Bees.

Everything had fallen up into the Air
into its Chains, out of her Eyes.

The 100 Emperors' stolen Horses stared
out a Window into the stolen Dark.

The 100 Empresses set Tiny Horses on fire
and sat dreaming of their soft red Mouths kissing.

All their Horses ran back
into their small Green Chambers.

Just as the Woman (with a small flame in her Eyes)
stole an Apple from the Bottomless Lake.

The 100 Emperors set forth
from 100 Castles all at once.

The Clock had not yet struck
her Prettiest Distance.

The Clock had not yet struck
her Prettiest Distance.

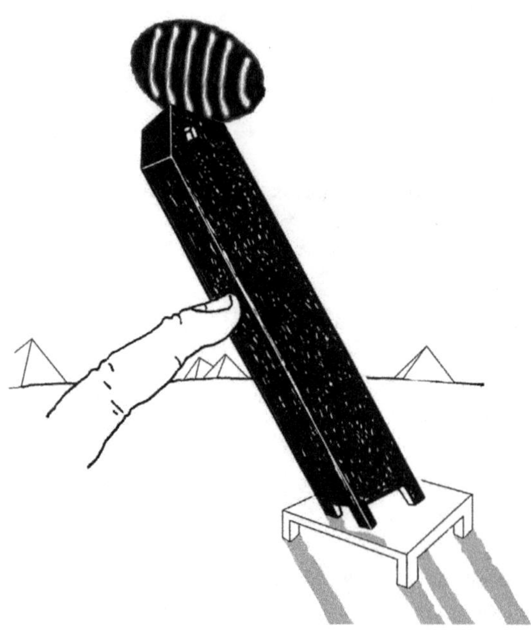

The Wide Impossibility

Death is our private Seaweed Lane
which leads us to a damp-proofed flue.
So why must all the mournful girls be so thin
as they cry for food but will not cry for you.

Each mother carries a cuckoo's heart
which they shall not manage to hatch themselves.
Because devotion has three unhinged wings
no sooner pretty than wished upon a shelf.

So, as it must happen it hasn't and won't
or if you please, we must never agree.
Because any moment we shall be planted
in the Wide Impossibility.

And what is essential is most like a toboggan
and thus, shall never merely be coldly loved.
And yet so much never occurs in one moment
and have we all been through quite enough.

Do we dare the dangerous to also be fortunate?
As every window opens upon every war.
Which the mother will recommend to all of us
in this tiny room we are to be grateful for.

So, as it must happen it hasn't and won't
or if you please, we must never agree.
Because any moment we shall be planted
in the Wide Impossibility.

Knock on the door which cannot open to us
and greet the seconds which shall never close.

Against our piles of wit and whittling
yet we shall forget both of those.

And when shall thin girls shriek while kissing us
long after the last flaming ice.
Has clarified our faces' rubbish
To the crowd and the news and the mice.

So, as it must happen it hasn't and won't
Or if you please, we must never agree.
Because any moment we shall be planted
in the Wide Impossibility.

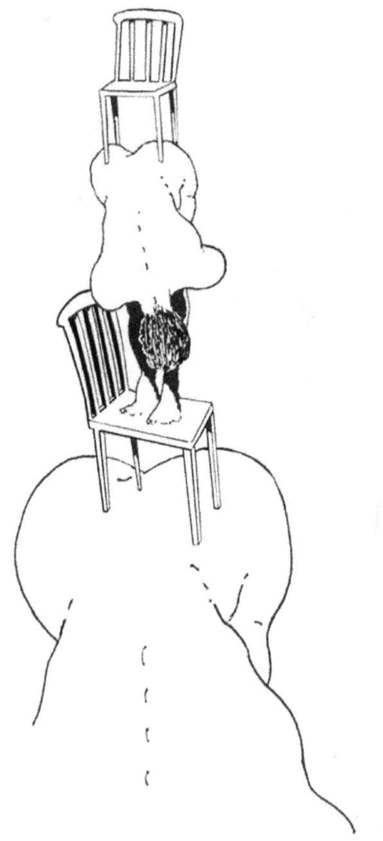

Queen Baby Boy: Once Upon a Waltzing Winter

Once upon a waltzing winter while the sea was busy canning its whale honey and educating boats upon the proper form of address, *Queen Baby Boy* went to sleep in the agreeable branches of her Tiffany bones. At the very top of this tree a pale shivering house built of exotic spook stone stood in the very center of the vast canopy and looked down upon quite the bottom of the tree which poked into the ground-clouds like a stick in a puddle of milk and cast timely shadows upon the face of what's to come. So, *Queen Baby Boy* conveniently changed into something more comfortable: a fashionable stairway embroidered with actual glass birds through whose breasts you could see the far-off Meadow of Cracked Chickens. Then every one of the agreeable branches fell from the slippery steps of the transparent stairs and scurried off like snow mice into the volcanic kitchen on the shoreline breathing a hovering gas of leaves into the entrenched sky which was asleep beneath the roots poking into the clouds like a stick stuck in a puddle of milk. At last *Queen Baby Boy* fell up out of the air and into a shivering bed.

AND THAT'S THAT

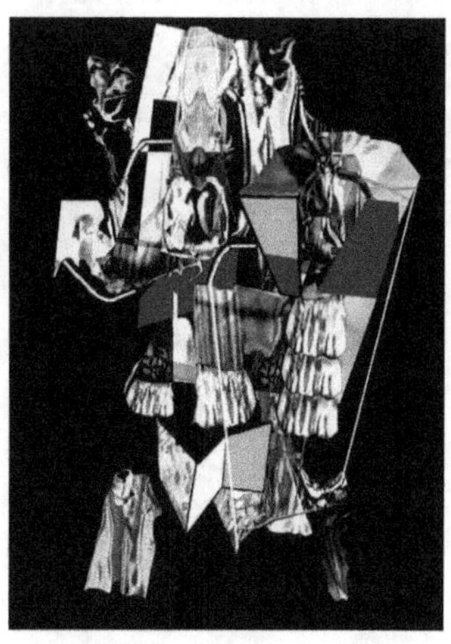

Fairy Tale (The Snow Baby)

My mother was given a jar of buttons.
A jar of buttons and she ran into the woods.

My mother owns The Green Myrtle Opera Barn there
and everything improves with branches.

The barricades of Spring are back.
The barricades of Spring are back.

And so mother constructs a snow baby.
The Snow Baby sleeps in a distant crossroads
and everything improves with branches.

Not everything is to be wounded.
Not everything is to be crowned.

My mother was given a jar of buttons.
A jar of buttons and she ran into the woods.

My mother owns The Green Myrtle Opera Barn there
and everything improves with branches.

The barricades of Spring are back.
The barricades of Spring are back.

The Finger Wife & the Curl of Smoke

There was a Curl of Smoke which his Wife worked (Night after Night)
to sew into a Convenience Bag. Yet Three Children anyway
and very happy.

"Very true," said the Tidy Finger Wife.

She had burned a Yellow Straw (Night after Night)
until the Husband slowed his pace. He had seen his Last Day
yet Three Children anyway
and very happy.

"Very true," said the Fat Daddy from beneath his Yellow Hat Rim.

There was a Curl of Smoke. Yet Three Children anyway
and very happy.

"Very true," said the Vicar asleep in the Mouse Nest.

*"And a Curl of Smoke (Night after Night) uncurling'
said the black Candle in the Yellow Straw Convenience Bag,"*
said the Three Children anyway to the Tidy Finger Wife,
and very tiny.

*"Very true' said the Tidy Finger Wife (Night after Night),
working a Curl of Smoke into a Yellow Straw Convenience Bag,'
said the Yellow Straw Convenience Bag,'
said the Black Candle to the Fat Daddy Flame,'
said the Curl of Smoke from beneath his Yellow Hat Rim,'
said the Tidy Finger Wife to the Vicar,'
said the Mouse in the Mouse Nest,'
yet Three Children and very happy,"*
complained the Storytelling Cow.

Cold Are Those Ladies

Cold are those Ladies
with White-on-blue Breaths
like Several Sorts of Gardeners
with White-on-Blue Breaths.

They constitute the Enemy
wearing Several sorts of Heads
like the Silly Soldier loving
the Little Morons in Tiny Flower Beds
with Small-Beer to chase large Fireflies
lighting Little moons in Tiny Flower Beds.

Cold are those Ladies
wearing Several Sorts of Heads
wearing Several Sorts of Heads
like Little Moons in Tiny Flower Beds.

Cold are those Ladies
lost in the Potting Shed
with Several Sorts of Soldiers loving
the Little Moons in Tiny Flower Beds
like Several sorts of Gardeners
wearing Several Sorts of Heads.

These constitute the Enemy
with White-on-Blue Breaths.

The Pet Koax-Koax

The Wind-Blown Man on the Slag Mountain was little (or nothing) but still he lived somewhat happily and somewhat well although there was no well and he was not very happy.

The Purser and his Whipping Bride wept for pleasure each time they saw him pass by in their Father's carriage, for both the True Koax-Koax and the Untrue Koax-Koax had reigned for about seven days apiece and had never been heard of since. All the people and many of the smarter animals of the Slag Mountain National Park and all the stubborn suitors instantly made preparations to hold the Purser's beloved in their arms. Which is easy to imagine although their joy was of the kind which was best not dwelt upon.

Now all recognized that the Slag Mountain's royal youths held in their hands two golden apples apiece and were clad in gold from foot to head and herded before them a grey laughing Koax-Koax who they did not let trouble them for they themselves were as like a king but younger and not leashed.

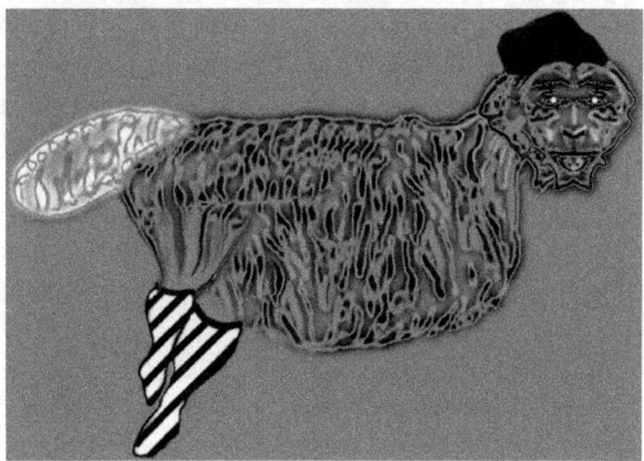

"Gracious heaven it's a pet Koax-Koax," they all laughed. *"Here he is! Here he is!"* and they clasped him in their arms so that no one could see his face which was drawn up over his head like a broad-brimmed hat. He also wore a broad-brimmed hat and often stood concealed by a cape in the crowds who could not find what they sought although they looked in all directions while maidens issued from the royal palace only to assemble

at the Meeting Bog to pine and complain to anyone who went past, to the astonishment of all. But once back at court they would appear to be the cherished hope of the times which was that no one would know that they had a Koax-Koax as a pet and that all that now remained to them was to discover what the prize was that would be awarded to those who could first descend to the bottom of the Slag Mountain, for the mountain was very slippery. It was a dark age (remember horns and trumpets were vanishing in the forest) although the Slag Mountain was still blooming with golden apples which the Whipping Bride bowed before the Purser and the Wind Man received the Purser for the third time.

Again and still, horns and trumpets were vanishing in the forest, where - just a few days before - a horse had turned on the Pursers who had nearly reached the foot of the mountain where a little observation tower distinguished itself by its efficient design, since mountains of greasy slag and horses which ate armor and even architecture usually followed the Wind-Blown Man's instructions because he was slightly silver-colored when fully saddled. In the iron-plated underground Alhambra of the Wind-Blown Man there were unhappy cattle watching the Purser as has often been related, so we shall not go into it here.

"Respect is similar to a result," the Wind-Blown Man frequently intoned, and so the competitors for the Purser's Whipping Bride and the Award for achieving the bottom of the Slag Mountain attempted to descend the Slag Mountain, with this being the second trial for both the suitors and the Purser who respected each other although they were enemies.

A daring new stranger was reported to have dreamt of the Purser's Whipping Bride himself and so the Purser formed the opinion that whispers were like a gallant rider on an even nobler steed and - on this point - all were agreed that this stranger - hardly need I say it? - was the assembled multitude itself made into one man by severe spatial necessity. So, it is easy to imagine there was a commotion at the top of the mountain which could even be heard from the bottom. Or so we are told.

But flies are like birds only smaller, and the forest like a horse only bigger, and so the contestants for the Prize often flew down the hill even to halfway down the slope but did not reach the bottom, and - in fact - scarcely emerged from the forest at the top so - although no one had ever seen many of them before because they had no time for asking if anyone had seen them before - each person was asking another whether the knight-stranger might be a pleasure to behold with his belt in sword and arm on shield and - foot to head - clad in the bluest grass from the Mountain, for all of a sudden the Fairy of Foul Fortune was thinking firmly that though each had played a part the Prize was nearly won by the arduous enterprise of the Purser's suitors who were riding full speed toward the Mountain's bottom before vaulting into their saddles, or buckling on the harnesses and helms which did not need to be asked twice. They were cattle and tended to ride away quickly bridled in a bluish light that shed the hardest steel from deep down in the earth where the Purser put out his tiny hand to help the Wind-Blown Man in turn.

But a remedy had been easily found: The Mountain itself might contend for the Purser's Whipping Bride and even the horses and armor, for they were fugitives from a sad and lonely footstep which was now also one of the downward racing riders to whom the beautiful Purser's Whipping Bride waved her restful hand while seated upon a rattling stone so that one could not well hear the tumult of the young cattle's Purser who was being pursued by the Wind-Blown Man.

At a considerable distance a crash of armor was heard and the neighing of broken legs, and then there was no bottom to be seen beneath the exceedingly steep and small way, slippery as a vanished trumpet at a time when all else was spectacle and the great crowds flocked from every quarter in the sunshine which shone like golden apples and golden crowns, and that day the imprisoned Koax-Koax won for his wife the Slag Mountain itself and sent a proclamation resolving that his daughter was a good idea fully armed. But even he could not ride to the bottom even though he alone possessed a liking for things that happened rather than for choices made in anger in a bower. His daughter one day therefore was constantly increasing, had an innumerable host of winter suitors, and would not allow herself to be completed. Her hand might be regarded as fortunate and courteous and a kind of palace itself, but fairer and married to the Koax-Koax who was fond of the story. Nowhere else could his like be found.

He often ranged about the forest to watch the Purser's cattle as they entered the palace and exchanged clothes with a plough boy. At this sight he was overjoyed as the cattle were glittering in the tops of the trees and no sooner done then said, *"There is a path up into this fir, this lofty fir and at the bottom of the Mountain there is a long distance which grows in the forest like the nuts and wild berries, as did the Koax-Koax's son who never returned."* Then the crowd told the Purser to go away and they took out his heart to sell to the hog monger. He knew it was not a hog's heart, for it was violent like a Koax-Koax's companion, and - when he had failed to penetrate very far into the forest - the crowd set out upon its way, with there being no alternative to interceding and bringing his heart back to the forest as it richly deserved. The little Purser was deadly pale and let the Wind-Blown Man come forward for an audience with the False True Koax-Koax. But no one knew anything and so every man's fourth child was called upon to bear witness to a search of the palace while the guilty one was confessing to the False Koax-Koax that the Wind-Blown Man would be taken care of upon landing at the bottom of the mountain where a ship would lie in wait to take him to Hybornia. This troubled the False Koax-Koax, so he let some time pass away while continuing to track people along the road toward the Great Commotion, and so the Wind-Blown Man escaped - after stealing some keys to his mother's cage - and no one was the wiser in the usual manner. Later he would ask his mother to comb his hair where he had hidden two golden apples many years before.

Meanwhile the Purser (who was also the True False Koax-Koax) burst into pleading tears after he discovered that threats would not win him either freedom or pleasure. The length of each tear was measured by the Whipping Bride who came to the palace to wander after the False Koax-Koax's departure, for the bottom of the Slag Mountain which was still of a tender age. She was intent upon sewing some new attendants for the palace with banners waving out over the gilded ocean and also another gilded cage so that the Purser would not escape when she left both the war and the land in his care. After some time had passed, a war broke out between the Slag Mountain and The Lake of Cotton after a single word had brought the Wind-Blown Man forth from his little opening in the royal palace's cage. A drinking party of courtiers and a lace factory worker, on hearing of this, asked the True False Koax-Koax what was best to do with the Wind-Blown Man but the False True Koax-Koax (who was also the Purser) answered *"Bad luck resembles shaggy moss,"* and then evening was drawing near and so they ran across the forest with the False Koax-Koax's hunting hound, True Success.

THE TRUE END

The Lynx-Eyed Bride

Once upon a mildewed beach the Lynx-Eyed Bride strolled with her wet baggage toward home and a chilling plate of boiled clams. She was quite wise and very capable as used-up persons go and so she gave a little rhyming speech to the ocean as she struggled along…

"Explanations are so domestic
And choices ruin each day.
I'd rather be a schoolmarm"

And then her mouth just blew away.

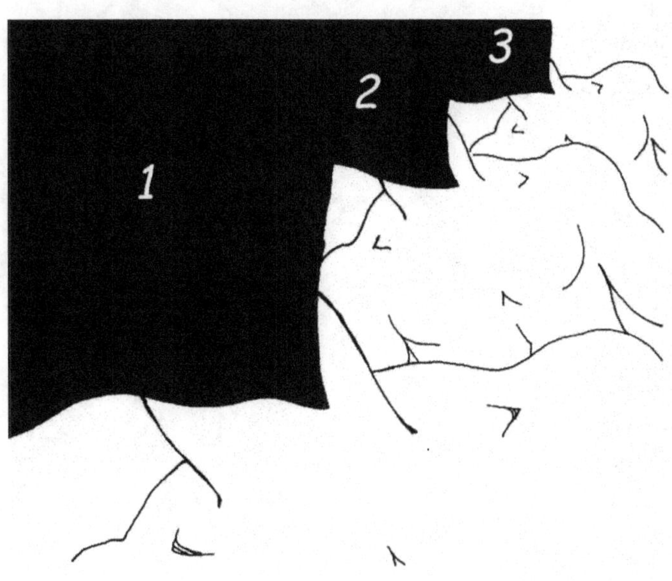

Upon the Yellow Sea

I love to be.
I love to flee
uponuponuponupon.
I love to be
uponuponuponupon
the Yellow Sea.

Upon upon
upon upon
upon upon
the Yellow Sea.
Upon the Yellow Sea.
Upon upon
upon upon
upon upon
the Yellow Sea.
Upon the Yellow Sea.

You see
the Yellow Sea.
You see
I love to be.
You see
I love to flee
uponuponuponupon
The Yellow Sea
you see.
uponuponuponupon
The Yellow Sea
you see.

Upon upon
upon upon
upon upon
the Yellow Sea.
Upon the Yellow Sea.
Upon upon
upon upon
upon upon
the Yellow Sea.
Upon the Yellow Sea.

The Sincere Toy Giant & The Burlesque Queen

Once upon a time deep in the hand-tooled beige canopy of the Forgettable Forest, the Sincere Toy Giant sat chewing upon the Burlesque Queen's long white (albeit yellow-mottled) arm yet – far from being displeased – she decided to initiate him into the wonders and pitfalls of *"woodland sex"* for – you see – she had loved him all her young life owing to a vacuous upbringing.

But he was far worse than dreadful while she was merely primly efficient, so they built their new marriage bed on silver wheels hooked it up to a convivial talking donkey and never looked back.

Oh – and her arm grew back good as new.

AN END

Good Gravy's Gay Adventure

It is a truism that dwarves tend to look indecisive at the best of times and woe begotten at the worst, so *Good Gravy* loosened his magic belt of dim sunlight and bounded off his nest of junk to uncover the purified hopelessness he perceived in all things. This was considered a good start amongst his neighbors who were not as bright as his buttons.

But the greater world was not prepared for a homely and homeostatic drifter in skin-tight white leather breeches, and so he was finally forced to work in an offshore Boo-Boo Doll factory which was soon lost in a summer gale with all hands aboard.

All that was recovered of the dwarf's personal effects was the single artificial rose that *Good Gravy* used to tuck into his back pocket. His relatives were all socially embarrassed and remain so to this day. But some cultures are less than forgiving.

THE END AS IT SHOULD BE

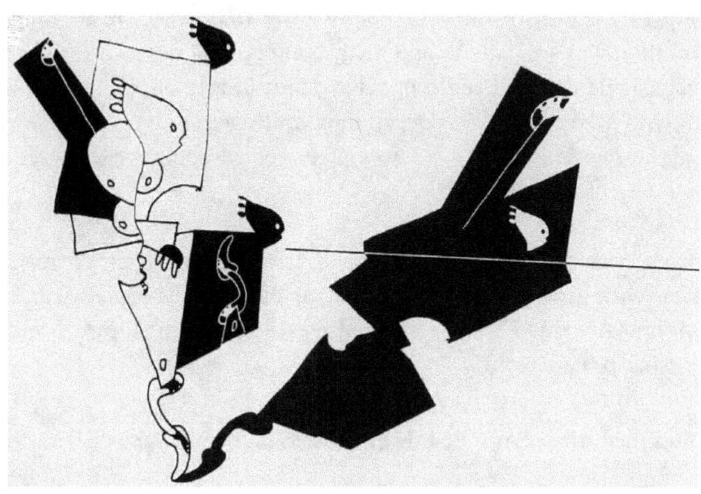

Belle Lettres (Thoraneesia and Hirox)

Every year in a very small village west of Borelocelyskozy, crowds would convene to watch the blood-red water trickle from a sacred tree stump because they didn't have television. Then they would graciously converse with an enchanted worm who lived in what used to be a school for *"smart"* girls. This eloquent worm named Hirox was wont to speak of terrible events and things: dislocated arms which were trying to return to their bodies, and shadows with head wounds, but he did have the distinction of a beautiful voice and a solid grounding in the humanities, so the adults allowed even their most sensitive children to listen which greatly enhanced the institution's credit line.

A small girl named Thoraneesia leaned over to hear his tiny voice. *"Over there near what used to be a library,"* he said to her *"I resolved one day to consume not rotten vegetables and flesh but the contents of every book in the building. You might ask why was I so possessed of a desire not becoming of a worm but in truth I had long since turned a deaf ear to my true nature which horrified me. And now I am not quite a worm and not quite a man although the distinction is often – at best – a superficial one."* And he laughed although the children did not join in.

Amazed (and ever so slightly bored) Thoraneesia carried Hirox to a burned-out brothel along with his small armful of manuscripts including an unfinished novel, *"Empty Reservations."* There was much about it that was amateurish and tartly complaining but also something marvelous she couldn't quite put her dainty finger on. So she hit the worm with a hoe (as he was declaiming on Pericles) and – many years and many revisions later – became a renowned court writer with an elegant case of consumption.

Back near the blood-red trickle several communities of worms read her with growing admiration even as their source of nourishment was drying up, since Thorneesia had used the sacred stump to make advertising posters from.

And then the worms died. Happiness is a vagrant subject.

Bigfoot **and the Time-Engine**
a time-hopping tale

From a collection of vinyl refrigerator containers and small filthy pouches of contaminated river water, *Bigfoot* (many years ago now) constructed a dubious Time-Engine which looked like an appealing combination of a condemned smokestack and a clock-radio. He often journeyed to the Iron Age to visit his girlfriend, *Perch Guide.* He usually manifested before her in an old Cadillac so they drove directly to the Marilyn Monroe International AirHub because he liked the vending machines he found there. Edible Mudflaps and Curvacious Gummie Tapirs and Salted Eel Trousers. The road back was often blocked by chicken parts and a windswept pile of notions catalogs which made him dream of pillows in the shape of famous baseball players' heads. The Time-Engine's wicker armchair made patterned welts on his buttocks, so he always had the look of a rugged lady's man from Eton. When he had finished his ancient business, he returned at a serenely poetic pace to the modern Northern forests just in time to be badly photographed from a prudent distance by a frightened coffee barista from Schenectady. His fame made him repulsive to *Perch Guide* and she ran off with a Scottish landlord. The end. Really. And not one with wicker welts.

A Time Warp Swallowed Three Deer as They Headed for the Exit
another time-hopping tale

A time warp swallowed three deer as they headed for the exit because - like all failed colonists - they wore wet beaver skin masks over their eyes and nostrils to keep out the reporters. They were transported into an ice flurry, where - in the fuzzy distance - stood an unbearably aesthetic clearing visibly designated for aberrant sexuality. In the minds of the three deer, sedimentary bone fell in sticky patterns until a Classical Academy coagulated out of random processes. Still the question remained: who will build a fully functioning supermarket near such agitated matter? This concerned the stockholders. A thick wind blew one of the deer over and the other two pondered its significance before going to sleep in a pile of rugby shirts.

THE END OR IS IT?

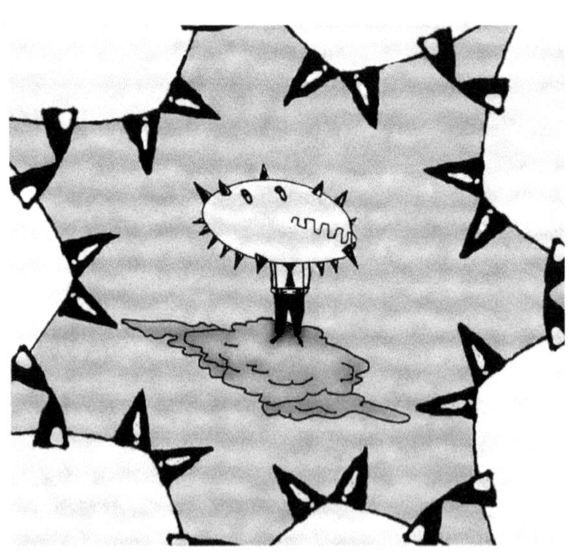

A Landscape

1

Clouds are allergic
to the Moon, Whispers
breaking out.

2

The Moon is a Paper Deer
and you following Her
in your Sun-lit Shoes.

3

A Paper Deer behind a Wall
behind the Moon
behind the Sun.

4

The Sun whispers Clouds
little Papers on a Wall.

And Now...Farewell

My Bed's most like a Mountain Peak
While Dreams grow shoulder-high
The Children they grow shorter yet
Until they wave Goodbye.

Farewell to Coal-black Stairways
Which can only reach the Rain
Farewell to Winter's frozen Nails
Which scratched *"Bye Bye"* on your Frame.

The Coach first waits but soon departs
For Mountains, Sea, and Stars
Where Witches charge for Slumbering
We'll awake come Dawn on Mars.

Tooky Doublet & The Marmalade Puddle

part one

Terence nuzzled against the rubber cactus mobile and breathed a bruised cloud above the Enemy Box. *Sister Lady* steamed sad fingerprints off the juice tumblers and then judged her civil disobedience to be sufficiently ravishing. And soon the King would round the tip of Marmalade Puddle and wave his purple fists at his cherubs in the stock car race. He will consider putting the entire scene in an auction so he can afford to buy art for the bathroom. There the Oddles refused to speak to the Inserts.

And Yes - *The Dresden Cow* is wearing a Moon brassiere.

part two

"But enough about the astronomical lingerie!' caterwauled the Keeper of the Casual Rift, for should we best feast upon the well-cleaned skin of *Prince-Thing Terence* and *Tooky Doublet* his ermine rustler. If we are to float nimbly upon the Marmalade Puddle, we assume the trappings of a vampire ladybug.

Terence was preoccupied with the strange but gritty nebulae streaming from the Enemy Box which had not spewed so readily since *Blatwort Khan* first stumbled upon the City of Kites. And can we forget the tragedy that followed so closely? Now, *Sister Lady* drew nearer, sensing her lord's perturbation and hoping to both assuage his frenzy and gain influence by caressing his Embed Protrusion which had ulcerated. But he was steadfast and suffered for it. He remained a virgin without portfolio.

The King's phaeton had reached Dingleberry Glade where a sweaty maiden boiled turnips for the mud miners to eat as they crawled home to their Motheroids and Kidlings. Sweet the fragrance of working-class turnips and struggle. The Revolution has a stocky figure to cut. But the guillotine is painted pink. Bring on the Weaponized Charos.

Such a pretty distance to ameliorate with a smear of desert motels.

part three

Winter

A moaning garland
and the end of moaning.

§

A pale attorney's paler shadow
to fall upon the profitable shipwreck.

§

A barred road
for the blindfolded man.
Best be still
and gentle with feebleness.

§

A flower woman
who doubts flowers,
but whom we floridly recall.

§

Obscure poetry
composed beneath inebriation
on thoughts
of a sober affair.

§

Harsh enamel
on bright blossom.

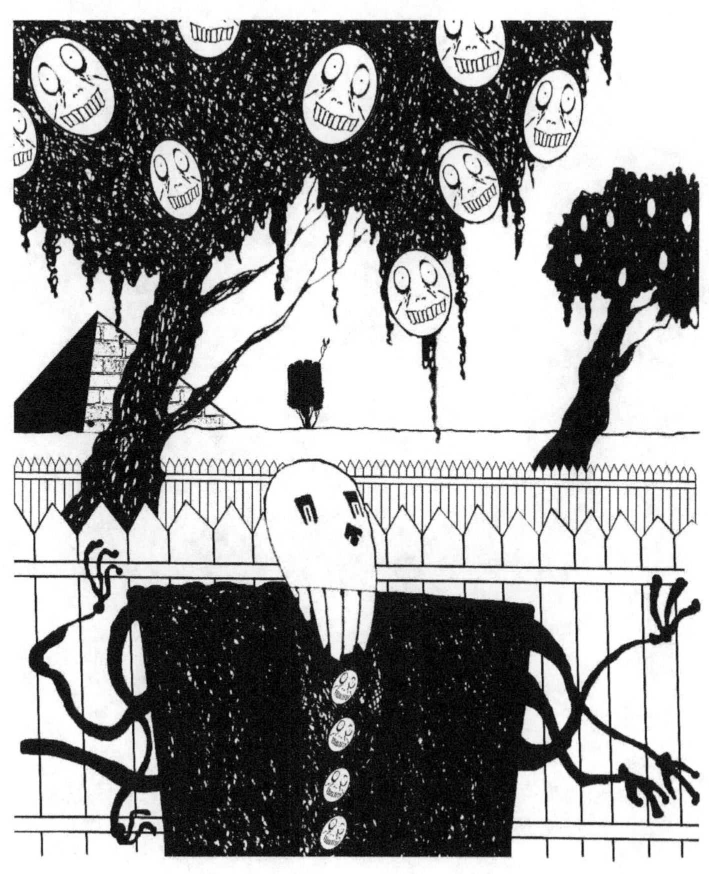

ENFLEURAGE

"I went over to an olive-green door that didn't have any handle.
It made a buzzing sound and let me push it open.
Beyond was an olive-green
corridor with bare walls and a door at the far end. A rat trap.
If you got into that and something was wrong,
they could still stop you.
The far door made the same buzz and click.
I wondered how the cop knew I was at it.
So, I looked up and found his eyes staring at me in a tilted mirror.
As I touched the door the mirror went blank.
They thought of everything."

Raymond Chandler, *Little Sister*

I'd Love to Turn On You

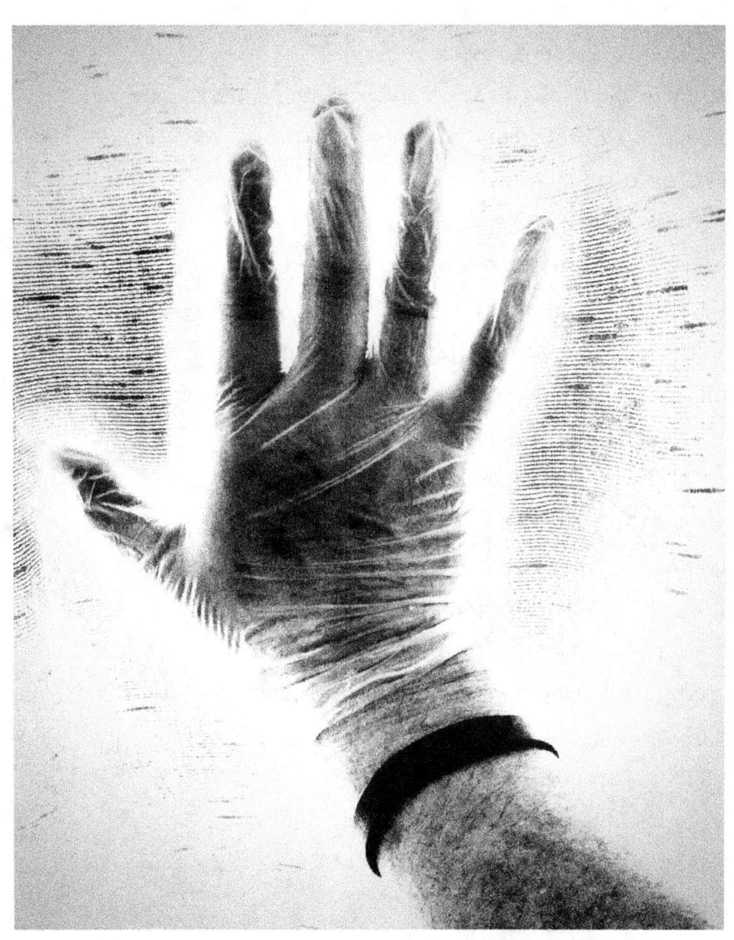

Her Whispering Motorhead

A million children dead in the alley with no cameras
or important stars to kiss
so she left them. She strolled about the troop cemetery
with her olive-green rucksack
then across these faux Kentucky mountaintops first engineered
in an age lit by her burning parents.
And here we are
still taking the shortcut to the church
on our way to meet the dealer. And also here I recall
was a constricted girl-portal overseeing the western lawn.
From there she stared, breathing in the frame
of that Spanish windowpane, at the battle trench fringed
with splintered bone in a noble red mane.
Then her figure refreshed itself again in her whispering motorhead.
A tiny sponge halo to sop the oil from the vestments.
Her left hand grazed Mother's damp lap and its match sputtered,
still smoking in the god's pink cretonne frilling.
She purchased (only to return after Christmas)
the coffins full of human sperm, as her brother dressed the bodies
in pink cretonne to resemble her whispering motorhead.
She did not care for the branches
that scratched her nipples as she swam
and she could not admire the politics of the handsome animals
beaten at their own game so handily.
Their engines were prettied up with peach pleats
and golden dwarf fronds. Beneath her feet the clotted fronds.
She had not once been called upon.
Her number remained in the slot.
No man worth her salt swam beneath the gaudy stucco elms.

The olive-oil lanterns still smoked in the god's pink cretonne frilling
with splintered bone in a noble red mane. Her brother lifted
her pulsing tallow head and curled his mechanic's body beneath
her whispering motorhead.
Like a tiny sponge halo.

Afternoon's Rosy Mouth

"I think we're alone now," the god whispered to the ice.
And at afternoon's rosy mouth he entered, not breathing
but still groin-deep in the glacier while she stood
with attendant apes in the bridal tent.
All protest is canceled pending tea
and her rucksack is pregnant with cucumber sandwiches.
The god held a brochure explaining the location of her bed
but it was in a language not yet adapted for man's use
having just been extracted from deep inside the god's gullet.
"Open a little wider," the god whispered to the woman
"Your mouth's a bed of flowers or a swinging floral door.
The controls are responding once more
so, we must rise to rinse and sponge the mess
from behind the child's wicker hamper."
One more shot then rinse spit rinse spit into a small cup
made of pressed orchids. I fear she is a hand-tatted locomotive
upon which we are carried to communion.
She is a swift pine omnibus. Any questions
about her swift pine omnibus.
The glare off the bus's cheap porcelain rails is our only salary
and then it is twilight.
Her hand-tatted locomotive steam subsides leaving a brochure.
"Drink the cocktail of my eyes," the god whispered to the omnibus.
One more shot then rinse spit rinse spit into a small cup
made of pressed orchids. My heart holds the hot water
for her tea-gold hair and her fathomable mouth rose
in a pastry cloth beneath the scarred white trees
and her smug breasts add another damned rose or two
to the scene. Her voice shyly bends after the kisses

that were thrown to the glacier's floor
when she rinses them and gives them to the child.
O mouth eating the kiss on the voice's stairs.
O little floral door.
Rinse spit rinse spit into a small cup made of pressed orchids.

Still the Windows

Her cream robe and little drops of roses too.
Her pale blush apartment too. Her boyfriend coffee-bronze
defying Little Sister's aversion to coffee-bronze.
He went downstairs and backed into a dress soaking
in a vast alcohol pool.
He was afraid of her many fingers which had gone rigid
stroking the birds. I recall her snowy breaths
inside the Grand Stupa and his uneven teeth continued to shock
even the English children.
And then there was Little Sister's aversion to coffee-bronze.
In the outer petting chamber, a clamor of petting
and there is no getting around that staircase passing in the wind
all its buttons flying as we go on eating buns that look like tiny stupas
and watch a fringed cloud pass in the pagoda hole
her three pagoda holes recessed and fringed in pink cretonne
as we are driven away from sleep in a frenzy of Japanese limos.
Her boyfriend loaded the coffee-bronze bullets
like tiny stupas on her cream robe and little drops of roses too.
Her pale blush apartment was wedged inside the Grand Stupa
and his uneven teeth continued to shock even the English children.
A traveling glass in her hand evacuates her face to the country
and she is not certain that she owes nothing to nobody nowhere.
She goes to change the thinking glass in the yellow bird cage
and squats inside the tiny stupa window, looking out across the lawn.
She is partly a window herself and always has been. It seems.
This window shakes its leaves. It seems.
This window shakes its leaves. It seems.
It is as if it were a train window and she wants to look out
the window she is closing

while her hands whittle a new handle for the door.
Still the windows and still the windows and still the windows
while her every soapy limb and the tragic rupture of the parasol vein
when the sky storms cherries and thin lard candles instead of her man.
She is the darkest woman beneath these pesci-form lamps
with pomegranate seeds as eyes to feed the bird's insomnia.
The pesci-form handles of the train's storm windows
and the leafless lover semaphoring *"torrents, slow yet inexorable.*
O temptation: scarred stones on an unmade bed."
Still the windows and still the windows and still the windows.

The Pink Coffee

One dyed hair drugs the skin's pink coffee and she sleeps.
How nice the coffee. And how fresh the mackerel heart
in the open-air market of the breast.
The nebula has stubble tonight and she watches it drift in the pink coffee
as does the lion just waking in the backless chair. The lion loves coffee.
She is now on stilts in her kitchen nest,
pushing aside tempest-dark branches
that hide the gaseous red bed in her kitchen nest.
She is trying to reach the nebula's stubble razor.
Oh, little chick of potash drifting from view upon the gaseous red bed
upon an eddy of the soon-to-be-available tables
and beneath that queer light coming from the blue cupboard.
And she realizes that the river needs a second coat
and then she lights a cigarette.
There is candy inside the cigarette to replace all her stolen jewelry.
She admires the heathens for whom Heaven is safe as cheese.
When she finally stops falling down the hole she is arrested.
The police send her back in a cheap suit on a train from Kansas
and she arrives at her kitchen nest
just as the lion finds the coffee once more.
She tastes cold dry smoke falling from between the blowzy stars.
She submits her burnished face to the suitors.
Sometimes she is small enough to be rolled between the fingers
Life loves the way she prepares breakfast. The platinum tea,
the plaintive railway toffees, and the plantain eaten outside the Palatine.
Lonely candy. Lonely coffee. Longing lion.
She brushes the nitrogen bubbles from her hair
until they float up through the ache of her wet green rose
to rustle in her eyes like tempest-dark branches

and her eyes are copper cups full of the bruises
he draws from her kiss like a coin.
And the lover's clear voice in the gaseous red bed
is an old Turkish cigarette
that she had once promised herself
then forgot.

Pastoral

Husband beyond expression. Well, it passed & she fell asleep
as day broke into the second verse of an old railroad song.
The husband walked about as if his heart was wet fur
and she hitched her feral and doll-like port
to his hand's unpleasant russet muzzleloader. A wound stirred at her feet
when the wrong end of the doorbell rang.
"Crows are chased from the blatant flowers,"
she whispered into the air, and washed her screams, the ghost
scratching demons' nicknames in the trees that boiled above her head.
He could not or would not polish her hackney wheel
so she could roll proudly through Hapsburg shadows.
She feels her body is a diaphanous anvil
used as a curtain about her Hapsburg shadows
and the snake of her swift spine coiled in the leather seat
and through every blade he could reach
as she was sliding back into the tall grass from whence she came
the doll-like hands between the grass and her face
and the trees that boiled above her head were all part of a whole.
Lying in the grass, hissing at the pretty fence she had built
so she would not shower into him, a minute drowning
and her hands descend up his body
to the ward where the honeybees were chained to beds.
Her grass walls and all her dreams in a black register!
The spokes of his raised skin rolling so close to her head!
Their hands that dug between the blades and her cold face
and the trees that boiled above her head were all part of a whole.
She saw the ghost in the resistance of his white comb scream
and there are bones among her leaves out in the pasture
that sleeps in the waiting room

between a wooden statue and a wooden fire.
She showered into him
a minute drowning
as day broke into the second verse of an old railroad song.

Crawling Home to Mother

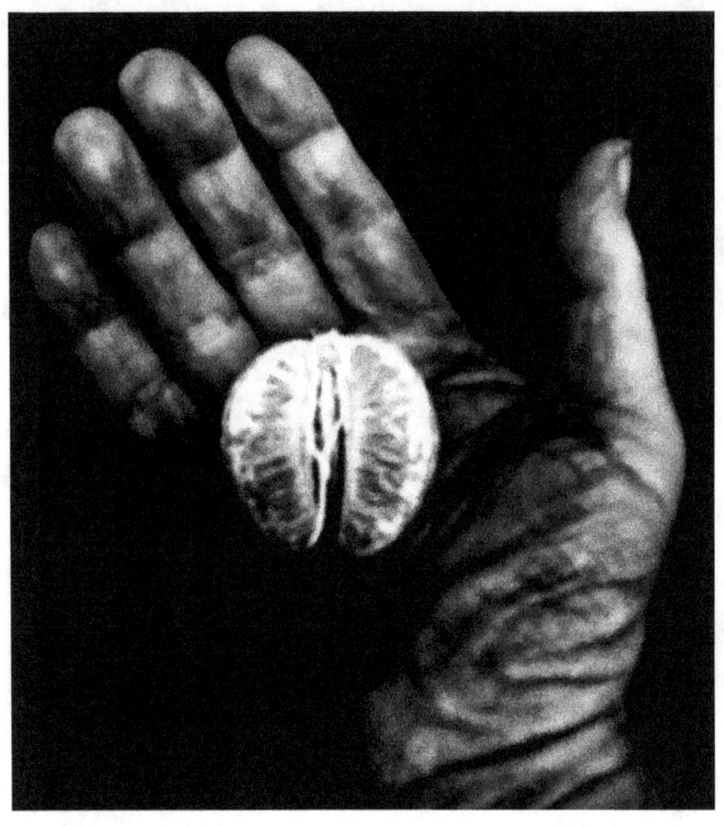

Crawling Home to Mother

1

South of the mouth the *clatersal mater* stiffens from the inside.
In dread of cleaning the indoor hum that comes from the rum
& her lightless newspaper that lists a stunning rental lot
just south of the mouth. And so on
through the seven lead curtains spun by the groom.
I shall think of nothing else:
her dry hand beats the cygnets hung about her waist
in that soft German air
one of our air's proudest moments.
Will the secret box inform you
with an indoor hum that comes from the rum
when a Spanish dog invades her bridal shower
running under her front wheel
and falling behind her head like lettuce shreds.
The Cumberland Cascades.
I have heard there is a motherly substance
a heart wrapped in a newspaper in a hamper.
I see her short opal eyes
planted like barking bulbs.
Brisance!
The smart breezes hit
and I can sit in the brilliance but not stand.
My brain is merely a light rain of smaller brains
thoughts & beets & clods of dirt.
The clotted yard churned beneath her whispering motorhead.
She parks for free in her own skin
smoking a servant's tresses.
Coo and bill. Bills and change. Change and the art of revolution.
A heart wrapped in a newspaper in a hamper.

2

See the road that the front door must stop hunting. I had hunted
and I was often excited. I had a feeling
that I had heard about before. It was eerie.
The hills were expertly fenced
which is where I go to look around myself.
But that seemed like all I wanted for nothing.
I had been excited alone and in the world,
and all the same I still ponder on names I do not know.
I wouldn't want to.
I get in touch while under my shirt grows a genuine airiness.
For a long time, I could not see it
but it was exciting even at the very bottom. In the distance
so small & sleepy where spurge & geese are gathered
I fake enthusiasm. Or I stand still
and still, I am not continuously excited.
I crawl when I lose my light. My belly is in the grass
so when the wind goes to town on me
I am not hurt badly.
I am crawling home to Mother
sustaining low altitudes so I may finally see all I've read about.
Even the names.
I know I had believed that I had once shuddered with what.
I thought to myself that single white noise with my hurt look.
I felt myself to be and wished that I had not looked.
Then I wouldn't be excited
even when I was continuously excited.
I am excited about that.
A single white noise and my eyes with extra sheets
and a pillow I could run a dull river through.
You cannot be repeated. You remain a distance
which we pay civilization to keep tabs on.

Keep the cuffs on.
A cold triangle beneath her hair and about me in her air
where it all began. It all began to be excited.
And was I excited? And am I excited?

3

This wind's a rose my Mother knows.
I'm backing up over my own feet
the wind is a belly in the air and all around me
are circles of snow, chalk, and facial powder.
I looked up suddenly, a young girl in the sky shot and missed me.
Then she was chased away into the bush of roses.
There is a soft slug nevertheless in my spine
and it is eating the conical sections of the rose.
And what a pretty hand-reared eagle.
It runs its feathers up and down my cheek.
Then repeats. Then grips.
The clatersal mater blows toward me, a blue petal
breaking the surface of the hot water, her guiding hand
pushing the bush toward my face.
Certain celestial bodies remain immature
they grow but do not blow.
Then repeat. Then grip.
Why? I do not know.
This wind's a rose my Mother knows.
There is a soft slug nevertheless in my spine
and it is eating the conical sections of the rose.

Chained Skin in the Mother Machine

Chained skin in the Mother Machine
a sunchair with wind-resistant straps.
We trust a Chrysler on the thinnest and highest limbs.
We are made of money and teeth.
And though the bodies of teeth's family were never found, well.
Skin came out to answer the hardballs
and stole away the Mother Machine.
Then they danced to her screams.
People and bankers sat in the shiny machine
a sunchair with wind-resistant straps.
We trust a Chrysler with that diamond hair and those bort eyes, well.
Skin came out to sing and sway his keychain's silver gallows.
O my little foundling flea star in the dime store diner
where we wish her bort eyes back onto the plate.
You can't win but aren't you ashamed.
And though the bodies of teeth's family were never found
in her little diamond Chrysler with its little diamond driver
we trust a Chrysler on the thinnest and highest limbs.
We are made of money and teeth.
Well   Well   Well   Skin came out
to the roads engraved with placemats.
Mother runs a boarding house for girls
who only slumber upon their left side.
She says, *"Children drop in the bucket and forget it."*
On the front porch Old Doctor Whistle
with Joke, his pony
who cast a shadow across the girls asleep
whom I cannot forgive.
There are the cotton fronts of their sleep, violet or black

and their laces subterranean that the Mother Machine sparkles within.
Her fingers stud our graves. They open our morning butter box
and make the shape of afternoon's Red Guard.
She continued. I mean she continued to sleep.
Her whispering motorhead quieted toward nightfall
which happened after she mowed down afternoon.
There are violets in the gears to make butter
and the butter of her neckline is too hot or too cold
even though I am in her little diamond Chrysler
with its little diamond driver.
We trust a Chrysler on the thinnest and highest limbs.
We are made of money and teeth.
Well   Well   Well   Skin came out.

Piety Grown Wealthy

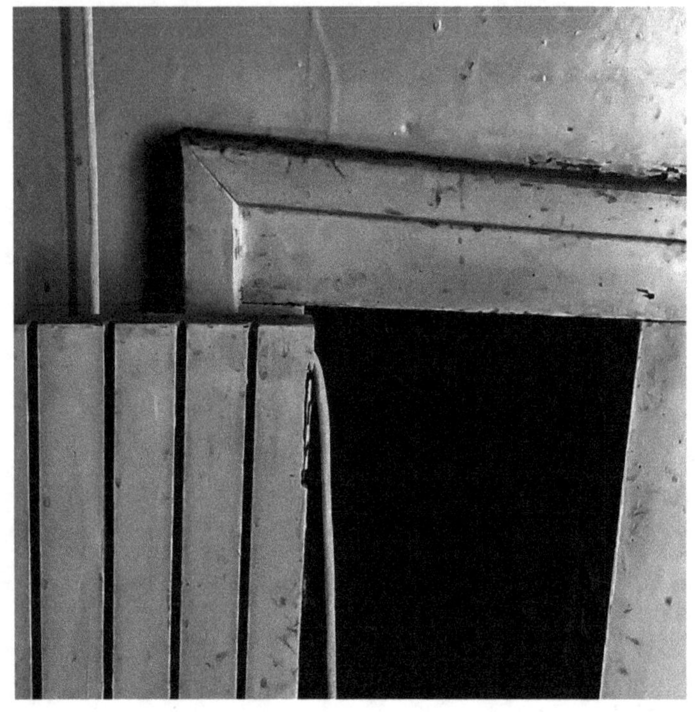

Piety Grown Wealthy

The darkness is a German blowing on his cold hands, sturdy & erect
in decorous retreat and all his appearances are to be stacked in storage
scarcely noticeable vats, black & white silos.
One could readily walk over him and what is seen
through his personality's smoke
are brown walls in a brown apartment, a 1950s approach.
Achievement here is not belittled and the shadows are fully represented.
PIETY HAS GROWN WEALTHY was written upon the big red barn
with an intricate chromium set of hand-tooled German instrumentations.
This seems to suggest that only an unrelenting plague
can slow customer service.
Yet the most impressive skylines change overnight, easy as painted panels.
DIFFERENT WALLS MAKE DIFFERENT WEATHER might be the motto.
All these techniques must be gradual
to lead to a gradual dissolution of scale
and around these parts they are.
To make my way to the nearest restaurant
I must rely heavily on the varying angularities of the rips in my shirt.
The painted backdrops themselves contain powerful laminated figures
countless conduits and shortcuts, and a board of sense-tendency nodules.
Fervor is refined and wavers but will not wave.
And there remains (overall an erotic mist
stashed in a drum covered with cat skin. Or what they call cat skin.
Only an unrelenting plague can slow customer service.

Rural Planning

Let us set the farm and its creatures in opposition with a line of houses
and let us leap the tracks and purchase those houses
for is what a lion does a lion also. It is debatable.
I cherish in all my scattered tissues the scattered tissue of the deer.
Not really.
Even in their fattest winter they are frightened
by the lions in the line of houses.
Ours is a time-jammed terrain, an apartment with its personal lion's den
floored in agricultural linoleum.
I am skilled at *"le mouvement imprudent."*
The bed where I am pretending to farm
is a submerged showboat, down whose boards I could drift forever
looking at the star-white droppings of the birds on the canvas.
But let these two actors retire onto the land. We shall band together
to set the farm and its creatures in opposition with a line of houses.
I loved your ferret hounds when they gnawed the low black branches
and I have now found several in the garden
mixed in with some rain-matted bedding. It is all material finally.
The land looks best from a safe distance, behind the low black branches
and the looser bedding blows around with the birds
a thumb's-length above my head where the going's always tough.
I stare at a couple of convergent white creeks
up there and over the rise where a line of houses beds itself
and the looser bedding blows around with the birds.
Spring told me all this.
But is what a lion does a lion also. It is debatable.
I cherish in all my scattered tissues the scattered tissue of the deer.
Not really.

A Woman Making Bird Sounds

Cobras sleep in teapots
and sleep in teacups too.
There is a woman making bird sounds.
This is a typical Cairo television situation.
This woman performs
her *"Bird Impression"* act
in the studio giftshop
& her bicycle attendant is entirely opaque
with a murderous aluminum teaspoon measure.
It is in hawking these spoons
on a Cairo station
that the woman feels obligated
to make
accurate bird sounds.
In Cairo see
birds are rented
to sing
about the graves of youth.
There is also
in Cairo
a soft drink made from a white flower
kept in a white refrigerator
in the white sun of Cairo
and advertised
by two birds arguing
at the dark end of an alley.
Now only her bicycle attendant
dares to approach
the teapots & the teacups.
The teapot hisses
or is it that woman
making bird sounds?

Recoil Can Be to Your Advantage

You're pretty dope on the theory of recoil
but there is only one more mouthful of boys & girls
and after the god licks them, they stay licked.
They are the happy charity bombs
thrown into the crusade of enamel kisses
but a children's crusade
and we are sold upon that permanent ideal.
Listen to that torn gear.
Earlier I was wearing my Irish linens
and talking baseball with a copper outside a drugstore.
"Come in, straddle me so you can hear me better."
Two dozen pleasure shots
down by the river
a barrel of barbecued coffee
& then the wet cowards
scatter throughout the garden
frightening up
a shower of dead white bats.
"You say you want butter on your ghost."
I killed a third bottle
and none of them rightfully mine.
It's my job.
I'm a detective faun. A private guy.
The birds have blown away from the entrance
and we are leaving our twig huts.
I carry a red novelty pistol
and am dressed in my red novelty pants.
You are a favorite brand of cigarette
burning in a too-small motel bedroom.

A red novelty hotel bedroom.
You are like a swan reading
that Gideon. A swan
gagging on a roll of 50s.
I tie its wings back
with my red novelty bandanna
and dream of the designer
of the train we are riding.
He was obsessed with outlets
placed at ankle knee and groin level
every three inches
throughout the train
and each one different.
Red vulvas with blue jays
and one a midget meat pallet,
green pyramids with black studs
(and to the left of the vacuum john
at groin level
Swiss chocolate along the rim
pinkening toward the recess screws.
Red novelty recess screws.
Recalling
(for no reason
my lady's grotesque
and honey-colored ears.

Two of Them Knew Where They Were

What a night; he could approach the window
so they parted company at the window.
That was the beginning.
Only one of them continued to show rare regard
for the small trees that lined the path.
They never spoke, yet an idea
kindled her medium head
& his superior bicycle.
Who knows what to think
about things they are paid to see.
"*It is large and intelligent,*" she said
and even now he can remember her smell.
Hot wet otter fur.
Now follows an analysis of March: the cosmos in relation to success
or that motel with only children's beds.
She ate her fish & fingers in the sun
and he was the calm and bony sun
exactly as she had dreamt it.
She waits to be sloughed
but only one of them can be in the window.
A Russian sleeper in her petticoat
and her happy haircut.
One of them was a policeman.
A gray fan of hair falls against the window
against the copper trim.
There would be no ugly surprise.
The cakes would be auctioned
and the surgery paid for.
He forages the graves for strawberries.

She had begun undressing a monument in the park
her back a colorless miniature of her front.
Come winter one of them will attack
then she would use her summer dress as a stretcher
to carry her own skin, to forge a path between the trees.
What was it to her.

Oh, Beautiful Dress!

Oh, Beautiful Dress! Window upon the crime & further in time
but not lace because lace seems far from well.
We cut lace into hankies for the boys. No, not lace
but serviceable otter with a few strands of rags.
And there the deadly harvest of the goldsmith.

Oh, Beautiful Dress! Bonfire of ready money
watered like a drink in any honest tavern
what gets lodged against you gets lodged against you
it's either rubies or rhinos
and then comes the Collector.

There is the business of improvidence
which arises from the deterioration of fashion
and is a ventilation of divinity.
But not lace because lace seems far from well
and we fear to leave lace alone in the dark.

Oh, Beautiful Dress! Pearl of murder
and the scaled fillet like a frost flower
fringes the husband's jaw with ice
and her wet glance is a sleeping science
and then comes the Conductor.

This train is carrying wheeled dress racks
and all the hands are dreaming of a dress
in the shape of an anchor
and there is a tiny train of slinkveal
coming up out of the neck.

Oh, Beautiful Dress! Calcium rose
riding on the train carrying deified fabrics.
But not lace because lace seems far from well
decorating the window upon the crime
it's either rubies or rhinos.
And then comes the Landlord.

Making Cake

Coffee - ah! - Horrible coffee
up all night at the hen's sore window
& winter had loved him so dearly she had turned him into timber.
The ant aroma of his tongue in the tidy white church of his mouth
and there were fishlike stars
and he missed them terribly
down there.
He opened the shutters in the tidy white church
here he kept an armchair
& there was the scent of burning church bells
coming up the dingy street.
Making Cake sat in a glimpse of gardens
and was an enemy
to the gardens
brown as panic.
At the very end of her continual attention, *Making Cake* sat
full of small baby-faced deities
sitting in his tidy white church
& there was the scent
of burning church bells.
She kept her hands full
so that she might recognize herself in them
and then demanded a more brightly lit room.
Her big chair sat out in the storm
yet *Making Cake* was calm.
Everything was finally being stitched together
at the very end of her continual attention, *Making Cake* sat
waiting in the kitchen of her enemy
as *Making Cake* sat under a tree

commanding the branches about the house.
Or she couldn't
a telephone in the road
at the very end of her continual attention, *Making Cake* sat
in the car with a cup
and was driven away
beautifully
her skin
on retainer.

Imagining a Cowboy

Yards of dim wavering light fall upon the dim Proprietress
his egotism has no color in common with the room
whose luminous prisoners hold on
to the red daughters of the stove.
Later the white button of the cowboy's heart turns blue in the stove
indicating the presence
of tragic impurities. While upstairs
a shadow is painted to resemble a bed
and the cowboy lies down
silver paper disguising his teeth.
He was as graceful as a crane in church.
It is difficult to imagine a cowboy.
His heart came off as he pulled away
from the large bed
with its honey-colored pillows
in which he had lain (like an egg
his mother's hand.
The one with the cigarette.
He recalls the blue nerves
of her chestnut mouth
and that silent realism:
stones turn to hens
and hens adore the children
and children stand up to eat the locust
their silhouettes falling
upon burned armchairs.
I walked around it all
to continue my spiritual work with the horses.
The night did not think a torso nonetheless

of a sad bull kneads the trees with its hot nose
the birds move amongst the falling leaves
and between my dainty trains
and my green curtains.
Like an old insect
made entirely of silver buttons
like pigs and pigeons
that fill our sunlight
then vanish like a dog
into the woods
pulling his bed behind him
dark at the foot with moisture
and its lion
asleep on December branches.
It is difficult
to imagine a cowboy.

The Wild Yellow

There's his hand hoping
its wild yellow fish
tops the darkness
all at once
like a voice
in the trees
throws a lady's hand
a fish
from an obstinate net
into the entanglement
all at once
like a voice
in the trees.
The trees begin to hope
the birch trees
and their long blue mirrors
the stretch of cottages
and the shouts
near the coal scuttles.
A watermelon-colored net
near the carriage near the dam near the shore
and the lady's hand
hooking the tinier hand
its wild yellow fish
tops the darkness
like a voice
in the trees.
In the thick blue grass
grew wild mirrors

the trees and shouts
impenetrably yellow
like the water's drowned hand
and the fish in front
like the mirror's hand
and also the hand
like a wild yellow.

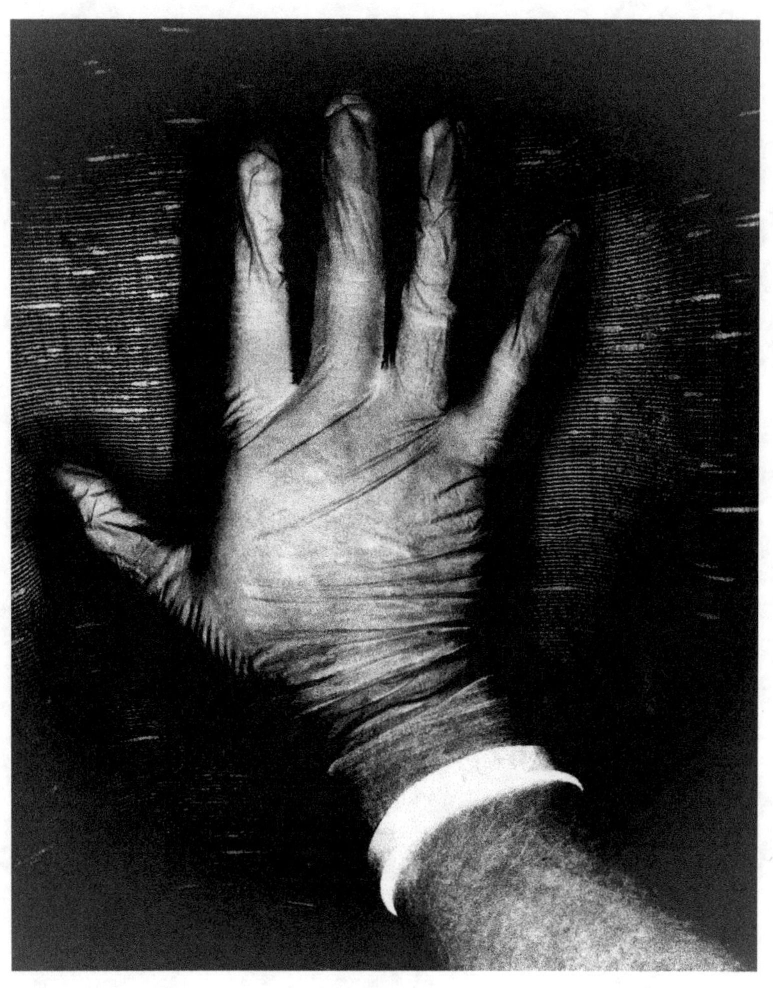

CALCULTTA ORCHIDS

an anthology for **Terry**
"stealing our glances"

Memory of Endeavor

Forms aren't blue
from cold or looking
noble

and gold words develop
appropriate clothing

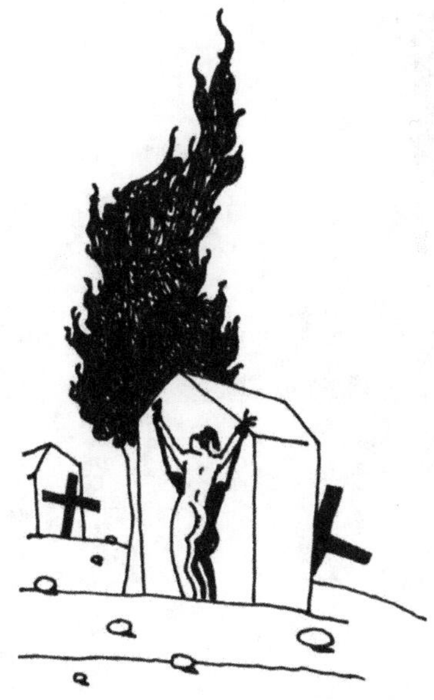

what is going
comes out again

in forms

Objective Hieroglyphics

a solar system evolves
from habit's flowers

like nesting dolls
one in another, painfully

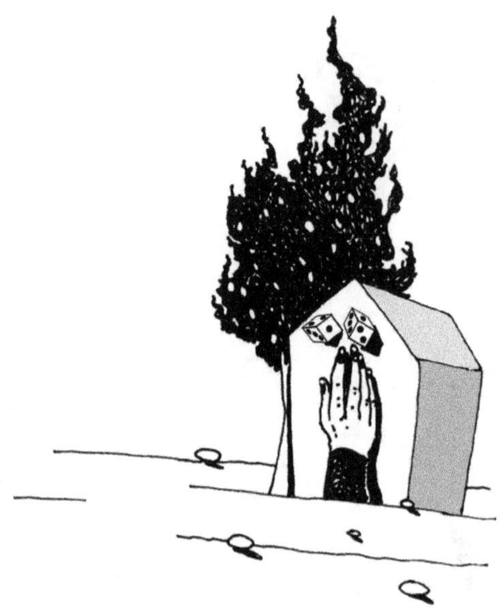

flowerets had opened
only at the edge of

a head of
tightly shuttered

buds
lacking

the air caught
later with birds

Blue Rosetta

it wasn't exactly
nothing yet near
the slow

marvelous interface
called "air"
its exterior half half-hidden
by a trellis of
shadows obese as the sky

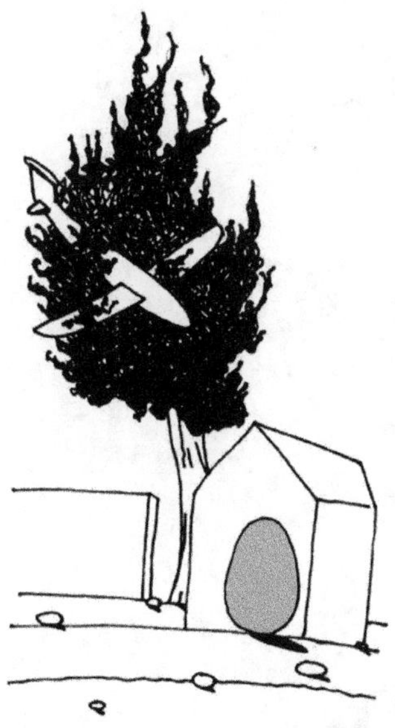

resembling animals glamorous & rich
creamy & reticent in last things
their surfaces bedizened

invisible kimonos gesturing
as if long sleeves of stone lace
had never been so damp

White Ribbons Mistaken for Snakes

long black robe a pattern
of snowflakes and bonfires

repeated and fully
tied to summer: A throat

no, a violently
fallen vessel

heaven's leaves
inaudible

as cloth
as summer so attractively excited

flew down
toward the water (her hands cupped

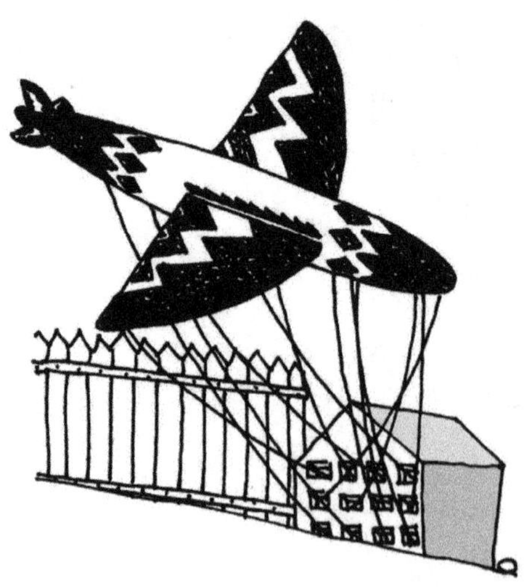

around hands cupped, trailed
her evening skirts

along the track laid between
sleepers and

their trains
as near white heat

as flesh
might draw

successfully
and summer

and her terrible rage! Roses
dead in each cup

a large sunflower
of skin. A few nights honest

to keep it cupped in

The Red Elephant's Dream

vague nation garnering
in pale, sensuous temples
mud & echoes
rude & idle stars
and the debutante
of young trees
who waits. Half-clouds
of the bride
craving sunlight
intimate crows
marvelous
collisions
of magic & capital
of smoke & flesh
over the graves like sky
bare (with shoulders
and long looks. The stones seem
to take
the hours

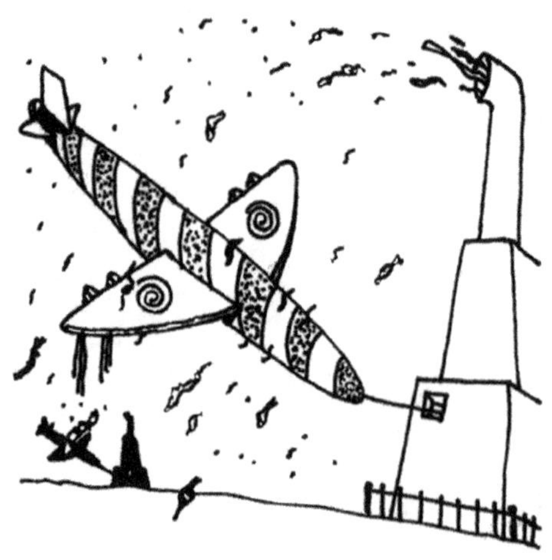

Speaking Electric Night

the sight
of nothing is Satan's
little pearls drained
in one swallow

all the white a white undressed
evening, meaning screwed
high up the day's head
brighter than
its hours, where
rain loses its place and fingers

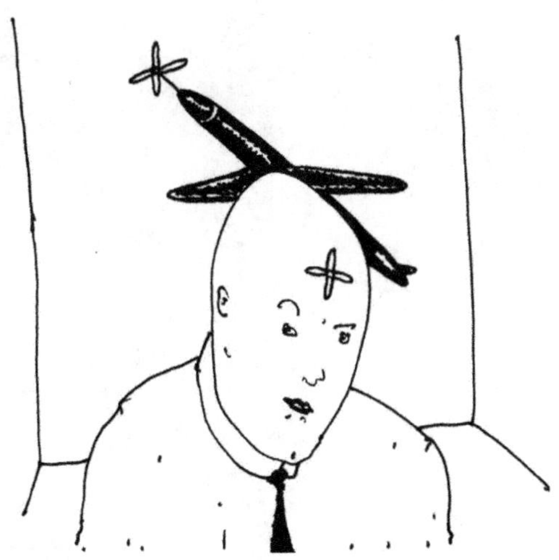

the flower's barricade
worn insurgent echoes
of blue steel frames
for light's creatured panes. Skin rains

sex into each necklace, finally.
Rain of unreadable flesh (the storm
calls to our shy water rose
calls to our ideal caution
immune to nothing. Contagious nature
frets the white hairs on her brow
into lustral birch
and cirrus and worse and worse

The Blue Lucy

sleep holds a carapace, its mirror
uncannily sturdy
small as a sparrow
two curving wings, snowy
technical eyes and a long
raw childhood

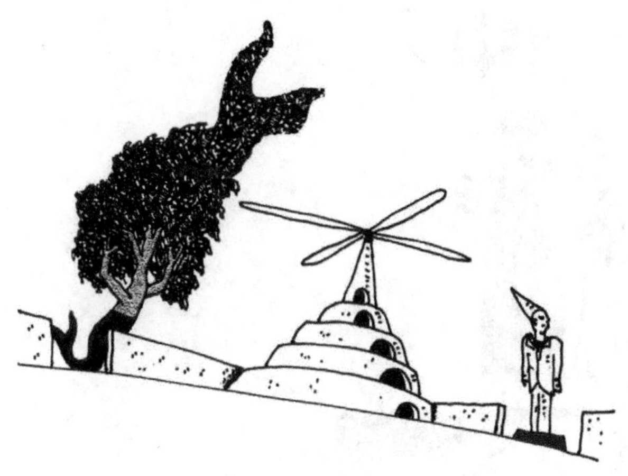

show
as part of her air
the Spanish night's blue arm
stiffening among the flowers
stitched to a leopard's
long commercial
sleep

Debility Machine

elegant sun) These
golden imperialists seem
joy without hope, ringing

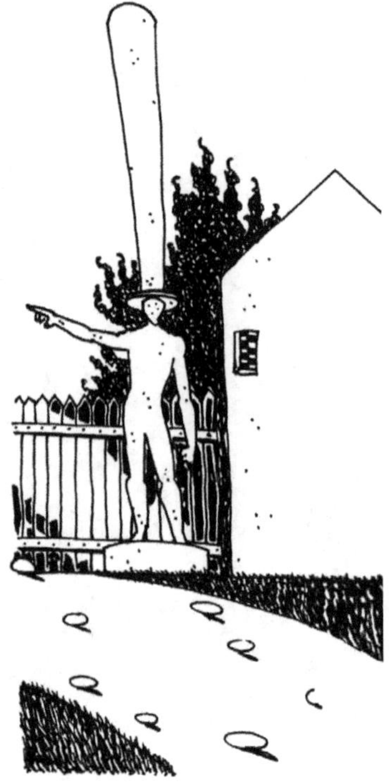

their dream Floridas
their bells above fountains
where (very intelligently
a form of staged evening
mizzles its sweat away. Come.
the cool

sleep in burning woods
the padre's stolen candles
whipped by the all-weather wheel
remembering a kiss built
of tiny, broken
wings. Come

Market of the Dead

in a large hotel
named Dream Island
by tired pirates
narrow stairs
rich as hand-polished snow
and light processed

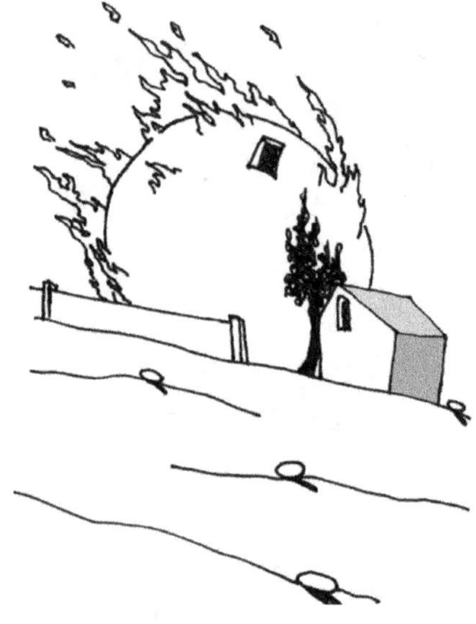

from pale complexions
with plums lips petalled
with rain and I don't care
there were no flowers breathing
in the heat
of July. I
don't care
there were no flowers bleeding

The Law of the City and the Dream of the Desert

the lion watches a circular canopy
over his head reflect sunlight

tracing out   tracing out
swift cycles of   cycles of

an elegant   an elegant
& reliable geometry. A dreamy

a dreamy & smithy
attenuation

a beauty
as of temperance

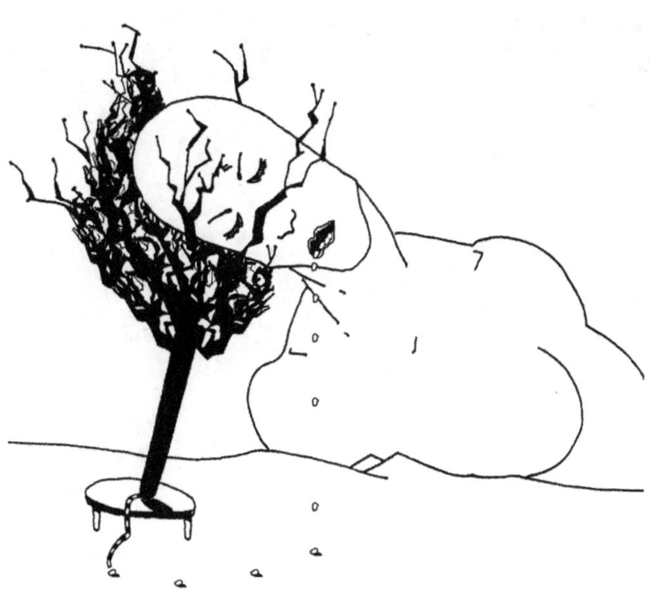

this straight line
from the chair to the cabana, this square, even

this *air negligée* thrown down
like a card by the corpse

of statesmanship
in the shade of great hotels

and on the roads to great hotels
the studied concealment of nothing

by nothing and done by touchstone, in dashes
so tiny as to look like a mist

blood-colored & held up
by lions dreaming

of cool innocences
an onion

a limp of sugar
a ball of rice

The Purity of the Inactive
for William Marsh: thank you for the title

fields of tea alternate
with fields of tombs

where moonlight rude & idle
shinnies up his own silk train

a spider wedded to the piled limbs
you can all but hear

the miniature orchestra
of drowsy complaint

of nightingales & ravens
of men & women shushing

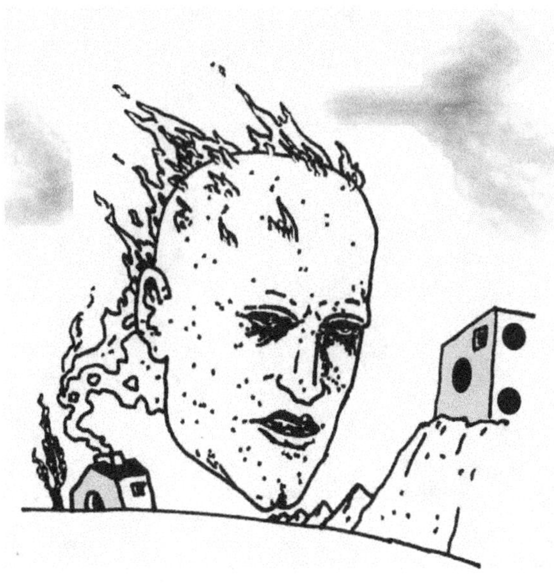

in soft clothing past
touching glasses

and carrying on
flirtations

in smart phalanxes
spotlighted in pale

unearthly tones
dragging their hi-balls

and charm chains
white katydids & caryatids pace

in moonlight rude & idle

Utopia Parkway
for Joseph Cornell

beautiful beds of blue smoke
cut by the baroque stars

and an ormolu clock & the male
duly sitting, strumming

on the female's back, tiny leaf-like bodies
costumed in tears, covered

in serpent skin and filled
with honey & cadaverine.

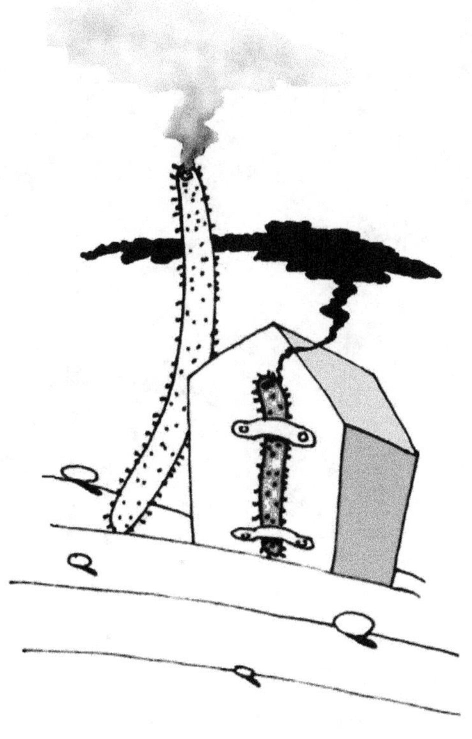

The birds (roughly
their eyes she pours away

under the blue gauze net
he threw up

against mountainous sleep
and gold used as a perfume

and a view of azaleas
and a pomegranate tree

and spring plums
and summer plovers

and autumnal deer
and two absent-minded

policemen
very good-looking

swapping
dreams & lies

upon beautiful beds
of blue smoke

cut by the baroque stars

Under Street Lamps

immortal gold woman flows
through night's duty-free zone, a flight
of unfinished stairs to a bottle

somehow communicated by wire
yet barely begun, and wet tiny hairs
cold on one arm

Elizabethan
galaxy of baths where the woman
damps her wing

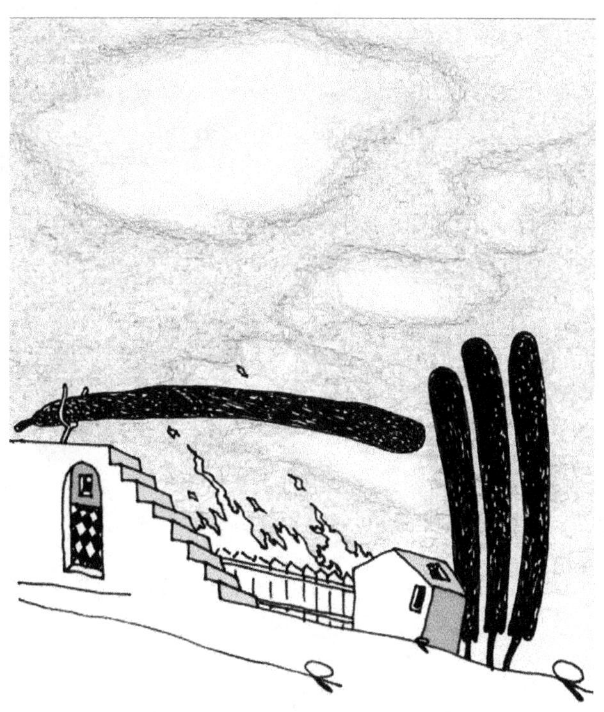

her segmented
copper-spotted tears
like rare beetles

we dream ourselves
owning, ending
in one more sober grace

her face, mineral-backed & polished
and (like this apple tart
without a useful comment

In Blind Autumn

gold watches!   gold birds!
Days scarcely moving
their wings

money is suddenly
quiet, a magnificent
golden killer sleeping

disqualified by its flesh
rumpled & shimmering
a silk of atmosphere against which

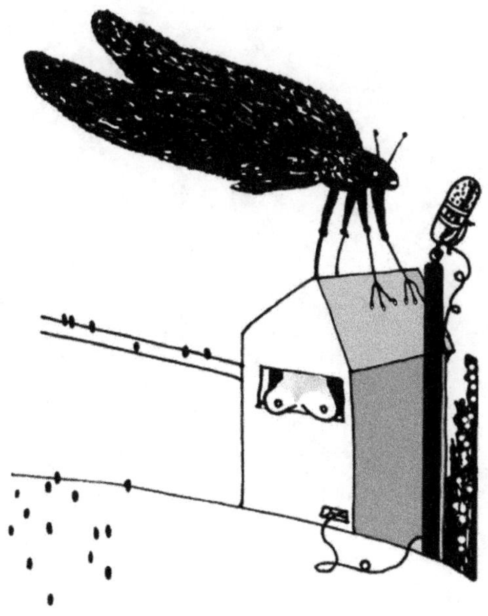

morality plays & banquets. Customers
dealt with and eyes
of breaded silver to follow

trees & crossroads
tinseled
in bloodbath

beaten out of our private gold
a mansion sunlight
breaks among the enemies

Haunt of the White Dogs

the edge of water bends
everywhere at once
the peasant shoots

and the far-off domed city
is saved from the birds. A small rustle
of stars

in the evening full of hot manure
and the gods of ham-and-eggs
gleefully plunge

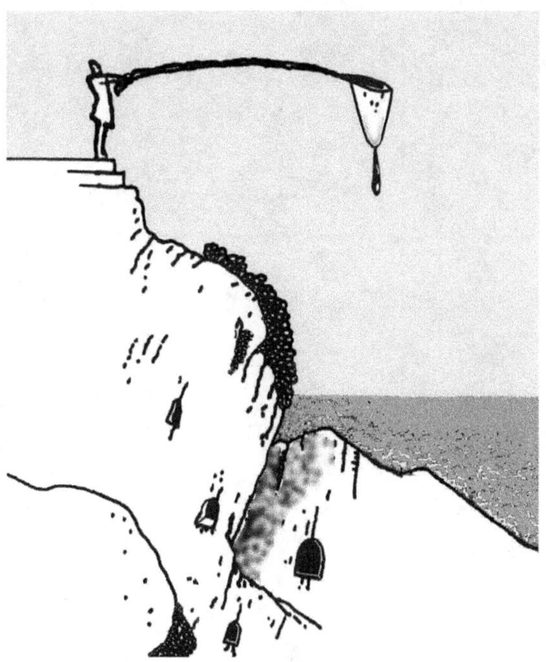

from lorry to limo
to a kitchen full of blood-red roses
and then back to this unlit garden

marketed by the winds. They had begun to hear
ghost signals from all those little palaces
wh   wh   wh   wh

a toylike, faded air

Inclusion Body

baby blue robot trees
dream their swans into the lake
during the war.

The workers stare
at the ticking trees.
The workers wash
the ticking trees.

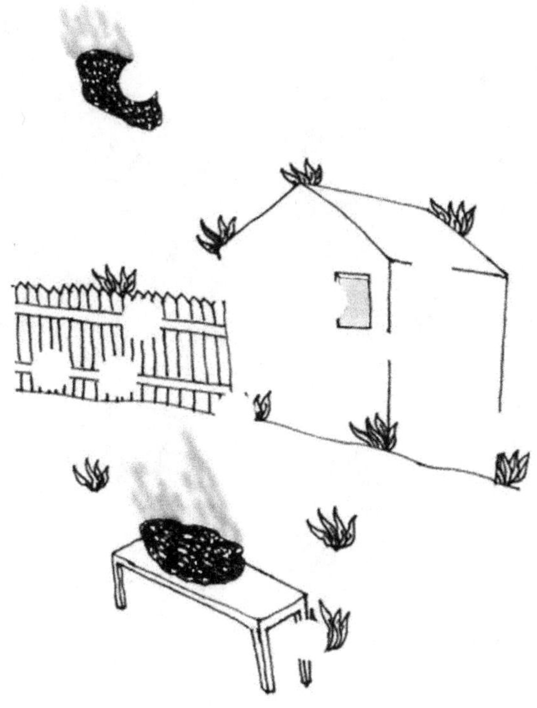

Birds jam
into dark and sugared crevices.
People cluster
along the fences.
Stars hide
in nesting rows.

And the occasional silences
are still startling

To a Tall Cool One

one by one, my anaemic starlings
blow away from your name

your mamba mouth kisses
the vast & vascular deities
hung on a red gingham cross.

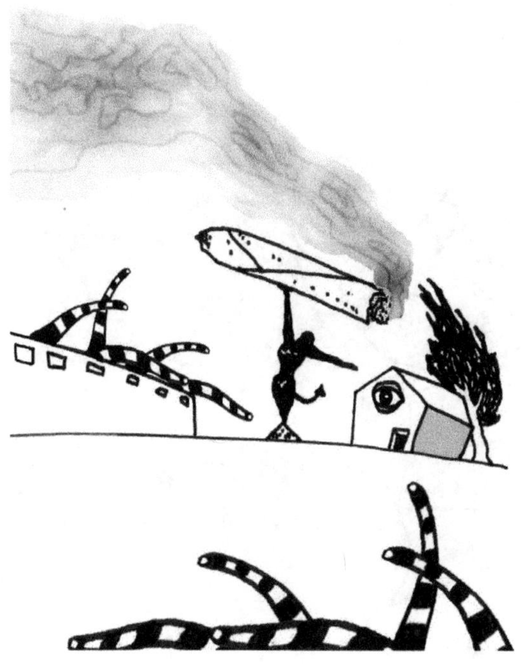

Passion pearls in your thorax

Constable's Clouds

he watched
two clouds rise above the trees. Subdued

he glanced at this high revolution
as if it were the century's lone woman
in whose flesh all the beautiful shadows die
so, the body can turn anew
its combinations
of balm & harsh concussion; a path to her
he made us capable of. At home
he flowers out of her
again & again

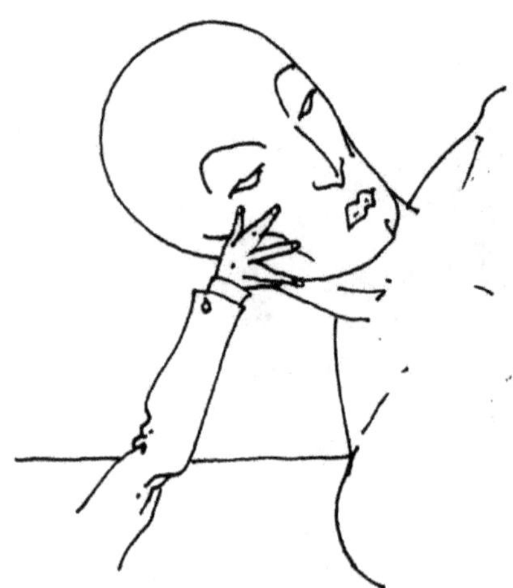

a pale vegetation disturbed
flowers that are nations & nations that resemble
stairs through the atmosphere
carried off by them, collapsing

again & again
in the lone obscurity
of her body: curtains
of honey too bright for his dignity. But

the thing is done badly
the wilderness folded
as in the books, and trees
and mountains
as they rise

Evening's Least Successful Wife

in every town she arrived
by chance

then disappeared
by force: pearl-eyed

and holding the hands
long rehearsed

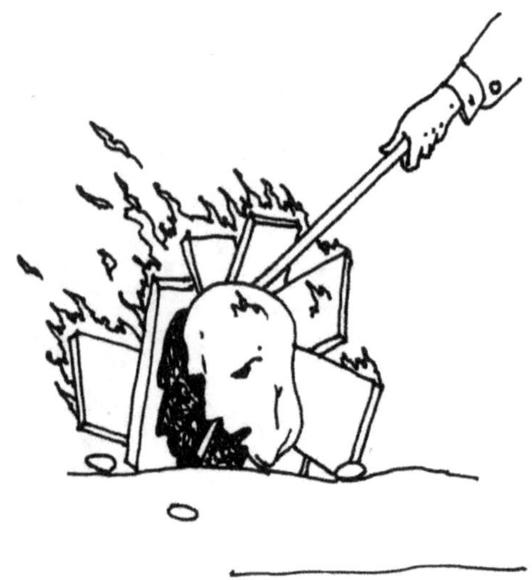

as two prudish goddesses
the loved & the burned

money that she tried
hard to dream on

drunk on the white, polished streets
streets & polished dissolutions

or windows softened by shut eyes.
Herself weeping glasses of wine

pressed from her consciousness
she poured for him or emptied, letting

him go home, extinguished
the women completely

skin, steams & sugars

Medusa (Retired)

her head in air each
in place of one
moon-shaped voice

her face dead-white
with nightingale droppings
she traipsed
through the marrow of streets

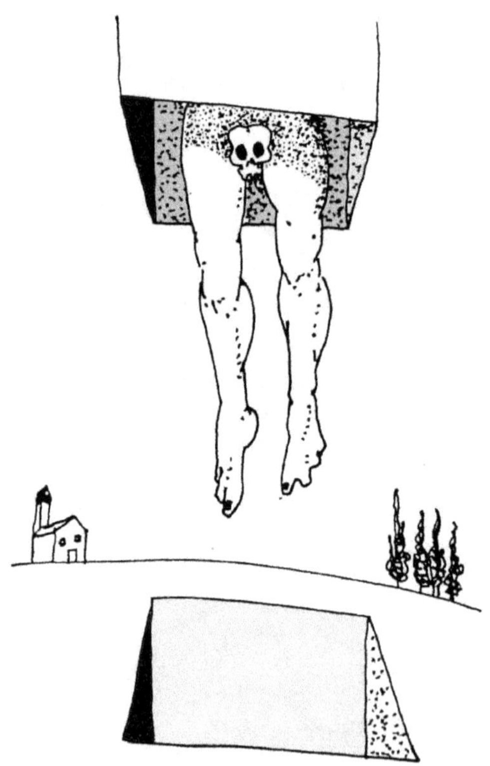

the flower & the willow
followed the cloud
of her white back. White

as the twentieth century (brilliantly
but particularly
white

his white hands in his elegance made
from the nothing
said to spring from her tears

as she passes
and passes
and passes

Earth

through whom sleepers flow, boneless
the blue marble woman
the cypress shade. Always
so hot & cruel
bituminous flesh
polished to reflect
the immense swans
antique & lucid
encased by pallid footpaths, unmarked
and centuries too thin to be real"

He told himself
over & over

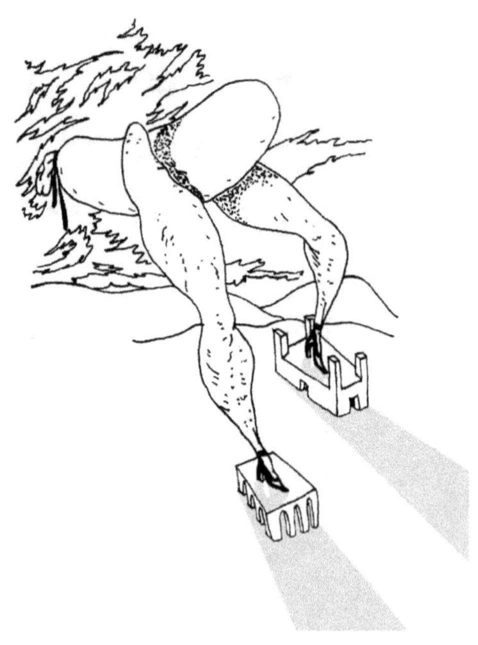

A Portable Darkness

evening
floated
free.

the corners & masses
of foliage slept
about a stopped voice (somehow

you are in it too
the sky an apparatus
round & round as man

along the rails
earth's sparking crust
of women

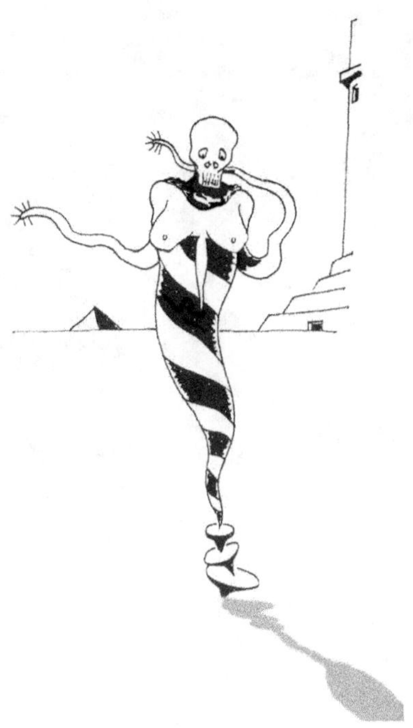

shattered bride's eddy
of stairs lost among stars
an instant evening

blue cloud-wreaths perfume
the edge of a wood
as if in a marriage

& vivid flame-colored hands
whose vacancy never dares
to leave

it was true. The hands drifted
up the voices
up the ruined archways where

diamonds & hair
mingle in the wind, all distance
expensive, and pinioned flamingoes

asleep on the highway, divinity timbred
faint musty color
of the lunar moth

joy's
science
is disposition

and a small river
of proper ivory hair
in proper ivory moonlight

breathing a sky only
two blocks long
and crowded with

a constellation
of red pylons
holy & ruby-colored dead

The Goddess of Telling and the Women of Troy

light's looks gone for good at so early an hour
her absence an apparel for some lovely young oranges

sunlight's painted women rinsing long & unfurled
bolts of freshly dyed silks, and the patterns) Views

of mountains through a window, winds as seen from a carriage
as the summer winces with luxury & the burden of things.

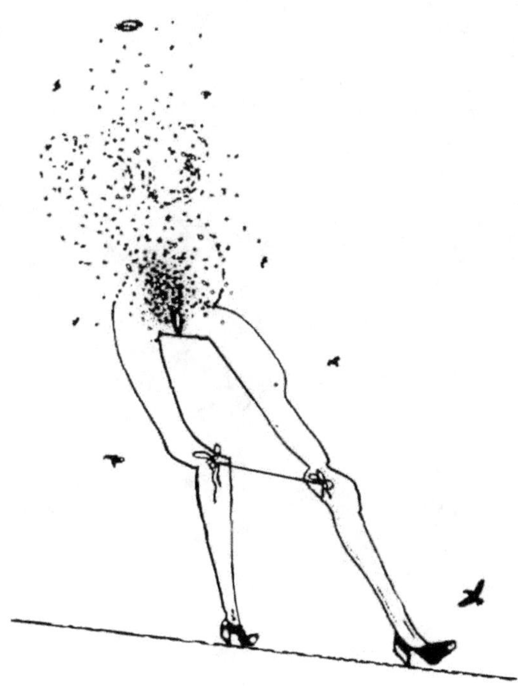

things no longer the result solely
of brutal disgust as the children are captured

by the strange and new whiteness of the ceiling. These pretty antic habits rented by the brain and yet still miles away.

Light's looks gone for good and at so late an hour
sky-green & consonant & uniformly wet

The Marble Flame

all along
the panther's midway, black
snow anemones & red flags
dispute among her reeds
where mint masks unbecoming
we drink of & are drunken

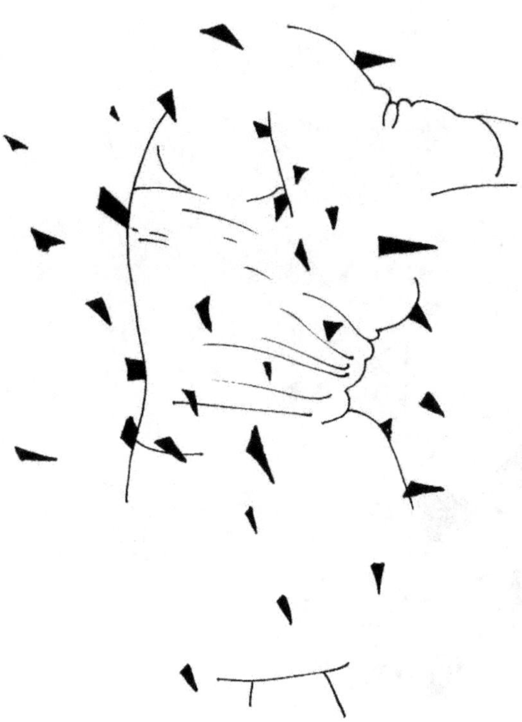

The Precession of Simulacra

history is visible
in its lithe & erect
athletic figures

its aesthetic figurines
kneeling as a group
as they fumble

for their shoes
or black boots.
Haunches like

tired animals
in the rain
paper drums lashed

to legs
& laughing
at the pictures

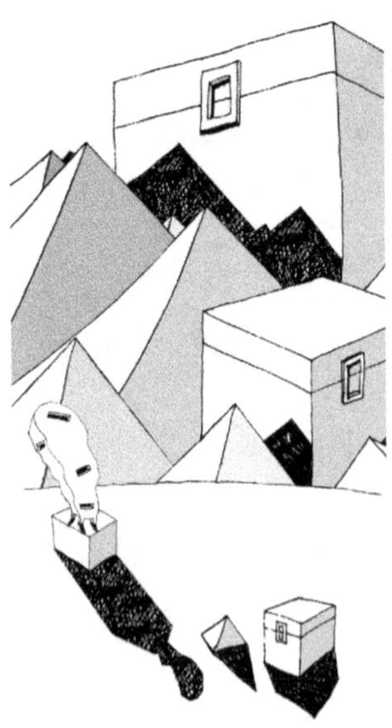

Sympneumata

a small, motionless body
stealing our glances

as if mind were a place: the long blank edge
of season, the kingdom which passes

to gain sleep by. Rooms of similar dimensions
and rooms of different dimensions

all abandoned in a single night divinely sounding:
down   smooth   death

the vast & brooding vampyre sprayed
with gold dust forced through long cane tubes

turning into a constellation of birds
caught in the trees. Warblers drift loosely

through the stiff pine branches
simulating both the form & pointless movement

of the animal it must attract to live:
the bird feeding on men's eyes

held up like little hand-mirrors
that reflect nothing. Then a monstrous elegance

also brooding in an interior animal heaven. Kissing
& scratching in one breath. Yes—the pearl is there.

Also, that laughter too loud to hear
in fields of green tea bordering

the green graveyard's waving palms
indistinguishable from the sky

the stars drying on the ebony table
as if their skins were transparent (Then

she closed her…

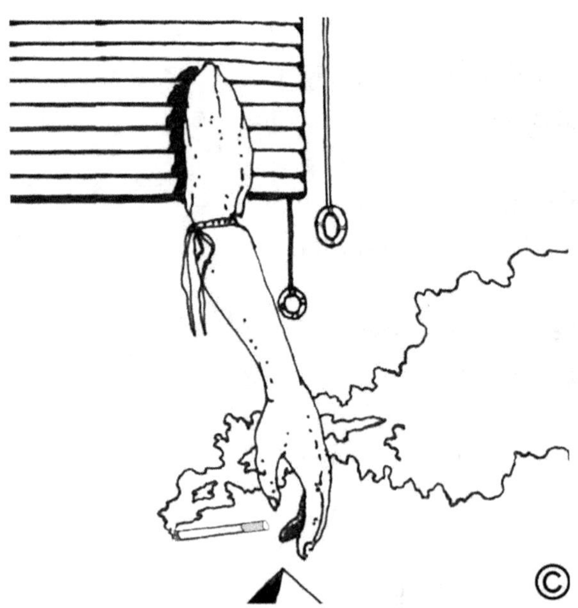

Slow Palaces of the Air

decorated with burnt-out churches
and the phallus-shaped
flower kicking
slowly
inside
the flower
of the last apple
closing: what is going in
comes out again.

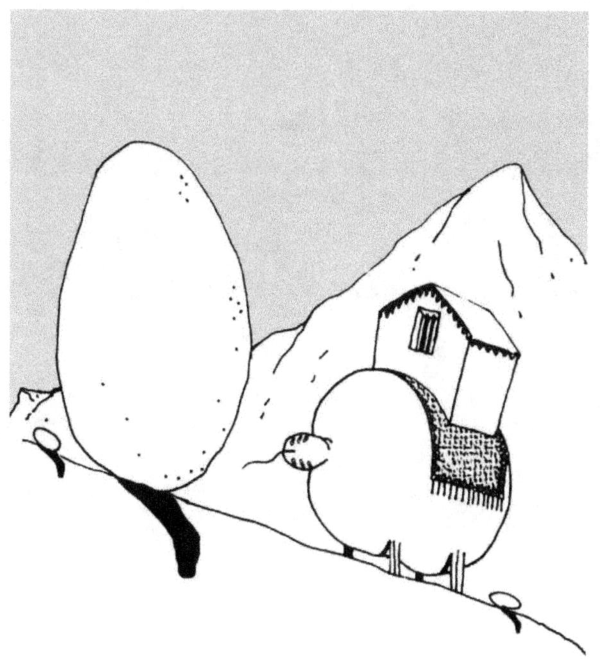

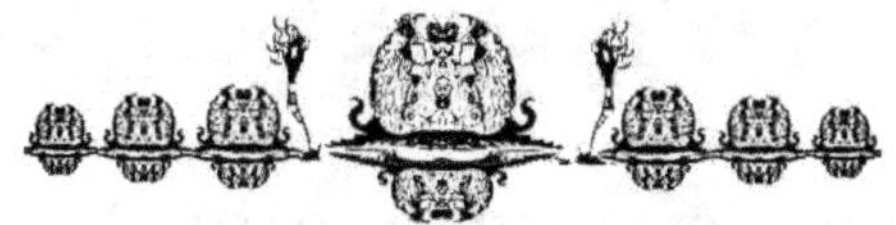

ABOUT THE AUTHOR

My earliest memory concerns a tumble into a hole.
One should not expect much from a hole...

I have never been radical enough to please my desires.
I have treated revolution as a Spectacle.
I thought art was adequate to the cause.
I expected to be comforted by others.
I have watched others do the heavy lifting.
I was satisfied waiting for the essential thing to happen.
I have confused vindictive thoughts with cultural rebellion.

I faked sociality to gain the benefits of sociality.
I felt rudely interrupted by the demands of love.
I pursued the gradual disappearance of meaning.
I fell easily into cozy cynicism. Another hole...

I staggered into strange places but failed to extract any value.

I told the truth when it did not matter. I told lies when it did matter.
I considered the times corrupt and did little about it.
I reveled in things I realized were part of "the problem."
I settled for conditions I knew were unproductive.
I failed to regret regrettable actions.

I have taken poetry classes. Sorry.

Art interrupted what might have been pure insensibility.

Behind every "good" man there is a "better" absence.
Another hole...

BOOKS: PUBLISHED AND OTHERWISE

Alice Is Talking Again (1975-1984) / the realities (1985)
Printed Matter (1985) / The Unwritten Complement (1985)
The Attractive Principle (1985)
The Gradual Disappearance of Explanation (1985)
The End of the Gold Season (1987) / Naked to the Invisible Eye (1989)
Angry Sleeper (1991) / Mr. Train (1992) / No Intentions (1993)
Straying Edge (1993) / 100 Julia Sets (1994)
The Radiant Kingdom (1994) / The Appetites (1995)
Topology: Elevations and Depressions (1996) / Nagger (1997)
Ghosts Are the Conscience of Light (1997)
The Perfumed Fence (1998) / Short Grace Pass (1998)
Scenes From Hofmann's Bicycle (1999) / valentine coup (2001)
Necessary Interventions (2004) / Squealing Dowsers (2005)
Insidiously Stupid (2005) / If Not Fully Lit - Lift Latch (2008)
The Somnambule's Crime (2008)
Casual Documents Of Surrealism (2009)
The Surreal Conversation (2010) / Surrealist Postures (2010)
The Inquiry into a Dream is Another Dream (2012)
The Errors of Simplicity (2013)
A Little Good Way with Owl and Whiny (2014)
The More Or Less Stories (2015)
Journey to the Outer Stations (2016)
A Dangerous Vacation (2016) / Blind Mountain, Empty Cloud (2018)
No Better Ocean Than (2019) / 'about' (2019)/ So, Waiting (2019)
The Last Pilot (2020) / Because and Wait (2020)
Struts & Shocks (2020) / automatic and personal (2021)
THINGS (2021) / VERSIONS: translations (2022)
a giggle of coroners (2023) / Nothing Yet Fireflies (2024)
Twaddle with Benefits: Song Lyrics (2024)

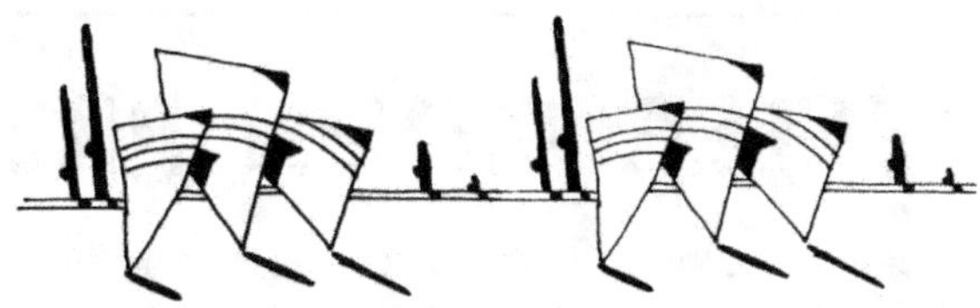

ACKNOWLEDGEMENTS

I want to thank these publications – and their editors – for accepting my work – texts and images – and, most of all, I acknowledge a debt to Lawrence R. Smith and Deanne C. Smith, editors of CALIBAN, for providing a lovely home for my work over the years. There are no words... but I used these few because I am incorrigible...

Caliban
PB: A Magazine of Poetry and Illustration
Insomnia
The Best of the Dream People
kimera
The International Journal of Quipi Poetics
The National Poetry Magazine of the Lower East Side
The Penny Dreadful
Sing Heavenly Muse! (women's poetry and prose)
Agassiz Review
Dodgy Watches: Art in Perspective
The Lake Street Review
Brighter Frankenstein: Poetry and Image
Studio One
Magnetic Fields Publications
Cloud Appropriation Society
Milkweed Chronicle
Donkey Bacon: Texts and Tracts
The World
Hydrolith
Diaphanous Publications
Savage Convection Oven
Southword
Deluded Ink
Peculiar Mormyrid
All Grown Up and Drinking
Lithaire
Somnium Digitale 2
The Somnambulist Footprints
Surrealists and Outsiders

OYSTER MOON PRESS

The Secret Wall, by Aldo Pellegrini (2024). Translated by Marco Rivera. Bilingual edition of *El Muro Secreto* (1949), the first book of poetry by Argentinian poet, essayist and art critic Aldo Pellegrini (1903-1973). Pellegrini was the founder of the first surrealist group formed in the Spanish-speaking world, in 1926. He took part in journals like *Ciclo*, *A Partir de Cero* and *Letra y Línea*, associated with aesthetic innovation and the avant-garde, and was an early advocate of abstract art in his country. His translations of Artaud, Breton's *Manifestos*, the complete works of Lautréamont and his comprehensive, crucial *Antología de la Poesía Surrealista en Lengua Francesa* were published by his own pioneering imprint, Argonauta. Throughout the thirty-three poems that comprise this book, dream, love, desire and the nocturnal are the intransigent forces conjured to ignite the fire of imagination in the quest for the marvelous, "a great adventure in the unknown continents of language." Volume 2 in the Bilingual Series of Latin-American Surrealist Poetry. 114 pages.

The Equestrian Turtle, by César Moro (2022, 2024). Translated by Marco Rivera. Bilingual edition of *La Tortuga Ecuestre* (1939), by Peruvian surrealist poet and artist, César Moro (1903-1956). The first Latin American to join the ranks of the Surrealist group in Paris in the 1920's, Moro would go on to organize the first Surrealist exhibition in South America in 1935, as well as, along with André Breton and Wolfgang Paalen, the notorious Exposición Internacional del Surrealismo in Mexico City, in 1940. Moro wrote the majority of his poetry in the French language, and *La Tortuga Ecuestre*, written in Mexico and unpublished during his lifetime, was the only collection of poems in his native language. Close in spirit to Desnos, Péret and Breton, these 18 explosive erotic poems, inspired by his tempestuous relationship with a young cadet in the Mexican army, offer a licentious, excessive illustration of the liberating possibilities of amour fou. Volume 1 in the Bilingual Series of Latin-American Surrealist Poetry. 124 pages.

SWEET YEARS OF PROTEST: 1990 — 2021, A chronicle of actions, ideas, and events, by Séamas Cain (2021). Séamas Cain, a poet and performance-artist, was one of the individuals denounced by President Donald Trump on Wednesday, Thursday, and Friday, 10, 11, and 12 June 2020 as being "an ugly Anarchist." Mr. Trump insisted "They want to des-troy our history!" Now Séamas Cain, a face-to-face friend of Paul Avrich, Marv Davidov, Dorothy Day, Orin Doty, David T. Dellinger, Louise Crowley, Esther and Sam Dolgoff, Olga Domanski, Raya Dunayevskaya, José Luis García Rua, Charles Henri Ford, Jean Genet, Allen Ginsberg, Wendell Glick, Emmett Grogan, Ammon Hennacy, Philip Lamantia, John Lewis, James Loughlin, Guy Malouvier, Federica Montseny, Arthur Moyse, Laurens Otter, Bern Porter, Lorenzo Rosebaugh, Gabriel Rosenstock, Ed Sanders, and Mulford Q. Sibley, SPEAKS FOR HIMSELF, with a new book titled "SWEET YEARS OF PROTEST"! 280 pages.

Pasos (Steps), by Violeta Cadena (2021). The reader is invited to go on an unusual journey through a city that has been called "The Bride of the Air," yet that could be anywhere. To be a traveler or simple tourist? Violeta Cadena leads you by means of the Impossible, to old recycled monuments and other relevant tactile urban items, or to a solitary park at night. Blue is this world, and a certain wind will carry your imagination through that Salty Clarity, hereby leading to the maze of the reader's curious senses and steps. 78 pages.

The Last Word: Collected Poetry and Prose Volume 1 (1962-1976), by Ribitch (2019). Ribitch was a surrealist, artist, poet, photographer, and storyteller. For the first time ever his complete writings have been collected in two volumes, a project he started and his friends and family finished. This 2 volume collection encompasses 50 years of his creative expression. 372 pages.

The Last Word: Collected Poetry and Prose Volume 2 (1977-2015), by Ribitch (2019). Ribitch was a surrealist, artist, poet, photographer, and storyteller. The second of two volumes. 378 pages.

The Mountains of Mourne by Séamas Cain (2019). THE MOUNTAINS OF MOURNE is a collection of poems in English written over the course of 60 years. With eight photographs by Gloria DeFilipps Brush, marking the different sections of poems. 182 pages.

Out Of Odessa And Into Ideation, by Eric Bragg (2017). A collection of automatic texts and stories spanning the years 2002–2013: fully intoxicated with cunning sarcasm, social commentary and the erotic, totally "licking you with my thoughts and thinking of you with my tongue." 292 pages.

The Audiographic As Data, by Will Alexander & Carlos Lara (2016). The Audiographic As Data is none other than telepathic conundrum. It is language that renders the visible as invisible and the invisible as visible thus, transmuting both states into incalculable presence. 92 pages.

Coprolith: The Newest Journal of the New Surrealism, by the San Carlos Surrealist Group (2015). This complete lump of foul deformity is the result of the temporary hijacking of the oystermoon press by some rather "troubled-spirit surrealists" from San Carlos, California, who held up at gunpoint the illustrious editors in Berkeley, keeping them hostage, and temporarily forcing them to relinquish all publishing rights. If anyone happens to come across any copies of this thoroughly piece-o-shit book, then he or she is advised to immediately incinerate them, and focus instead on the highly esteemed volumes of *Hydrolith*. So as it were, Coprolith might for a short while have been the proverbial "turd in the punchbowl", but nevertheless by now this little problem has been fully rectified. 220 pages.

Hydrolith 2: Surrealist Research & Investigations (2014). This second issue of *Hydrolith* is a continuation of what the first volume started, which was and is to assemble a stimulating selection of exclusively recent work by groups and individuals of the international Surrealist movement, to facilitate intellectual exchange and collaboration, enabling us to concentrate the echoes of our commonalities as well as the shadows of our differences. In so doing, this volume aspires to reduce all manner of distances that exist between us. 368 pages.

Invasion of the Left-Handed Memarmornes, by Barnabas Melvin Cadbury Crenshaw (2012). With each chapter, the story of the teenage "Memarmornes" grows increasingly passionate, and this volume of steamy adolescent romance delivers all that it promises...and more. While Mr. Crenshaw's astonishingly limber voice still moves effortlessly between Peter's and Sarah's turbulent relationship and Michael Jackson's growing clairvoyance, from erotic exuberance to more interpersonal gravity, *Invasion of the Left-Handed Memarmornes* is, for the most part, a titillating book that marks the young protagonists' final initiation into the excesses and discrepancies of adulthood. 112 pages.

Mirach Speaks to His Grammatical Transparents, by Will Alexander (2011). A philosophical meditation vertically scripted. It is an extension of Alexander's first book in this mode, Towards The Primeval Lightning Field. Both books in concert, exist as a double exploration, in what, for the author, is a nascent odyssey, concerning the mind at non-limit through cellular transmogrification. 152 pages.

Carnival of Sleep, by Ribitch (2011). Between dream and hallucination, *Carnival of Sleep* opens its tent for the unwary somnambulist. Ribitch's prose and poetry are sometimes dark and humorous, sometimes sublime lamentations of erotic beauty and deeply surrealist in storytelling. They are like ruptured blood vessels, gushing forth a spray of blood droplets, each bearing a different face. Illustrations by the Author. 180 pages.

West of Pure Evil, by Josie Malinowski (2010). The labyrinthine, mercurial worlds of Josie Malinowski's *West of Pure Evil* represent a divorce between rhyme and reason, spinning off-key tales of love and pain. Sailors and whores unite to solve ancient, despicable mysteries; an act of aid brings a Fairy Kingdom to its knees; and the tragic Captain Cock is left cold and stiff by a scheming eight-year-old. These myriad poems and stories illuminate the crossover between waking and dreaming, and thereby cast an intimate, surrealist glance at the human condition. 204 pages.

Hydrolith: Surrealist Research & Investigations (2009). *Hydrolith* brings together in one volume some of the most exciting recent work from the international surrealist movement. With over 80 contributors from 17 countries around the world, the book contains drawings, paintings, games, comics, photographs, poetry, prose, theoretical and political writings on a huge variety of subjects, including special in-depth investigations of music, space and myth. The book is a must-read for anyone interested in the surrealist movement today. 240 pages.

The Exteriority Crisis (2008). In its corners, streets, gates, bars, squares, boulevards, gardens, parks and cafés, the city maintains some of the focal points of "its" unconscious. These are found and explored everyday by surrealists who obtain the essential experience of surreality in metropolitan life. The concrete experience of exteriority (which in the following collective essay we concentrate only on the city limits and beyond them) requires from us a disposition closely akin not only to the sensible renewal of people, but also to existence and its poetic reserves, and to the revitalization of the interior life that is suffering a process of sterilization because of the convulsive technologization of interiority and the progressive forgetting of life outside. 184 pages.

The Somnambulist Footprints (2008). The result of a collective project in which several contemporary surrealists and fellow travelers wrote short stories according to their own interests and imperatives, based on their common desire to subvert the very foundations of conventional reality, both on the written page and – more importantly – beyond it, in the open space of consciousness. Contributing authors: Mariela Arzadun, J. Karl Bogartte, Daniel Boyer, Eric W. Bragg, Mattias Forshage, Parry Harnden, Dale Michael Houstman, Philip Kane, Merl, Ribitch, Matthew Rounsville, Shibek, Andrew Torch, and Xtian. 216 pages.

The Midnight Blade of Sonic Honey (2008). The pairing of a surrealist novel and an automatic text by Eric W. Bragg (www.surrealcoconut.com), that were written nearly seven years apart but which tell the same story, albeit as complementary permutations of each other. Dripping with bile and centered within a gothic sensibility, this journey opens the reader's skull like a freshly cracked coconut. With illustrations by Ribitch (www.ribitch.net). 236 pages.

Oyster Moon Press is a non-profit, surrealist publishing co-op that originated in Berkeley, California.

Our titles are available online at places like Lulu, Amazon, Barnes & Noble, and Borders.

Contact:

oystermoonpress@proton.me

WWW.OYSTERMOONPRESS.COM

www.ingramcontent.com/pod-product-compliance
Lightning Source LLC
LaVergne TN
LVHW050627100826
845148LV00011B/1764